She squared her shoulders. "We can't do this again."

He stood. "I won't endanger your job. I promise."

She swallowed and tried to convince herself it was what she wanted. "Thank you. I appreciate that."

"I won't, however, promise not to kiss you again."

Any protest she might have made was thwarted by his fingers caressing her cheek. The next moment, he was gone, walking down the dark road toward the bunkhouse.

Natalie touched her face, which still tingled from his caress.

If Aaron were a man of his word, and she highly suspected he was, she would have to guard herself diligently.

A girl could only resist the man of her dreams for so long.

Dear Reader,

We hope you already know that Harlequin American Romance publishes heartwarming stories about the comforts of home and the joys of family. To celebrate our 25th year of publishing great books, we're pleased to present a special miniseries that sings the praises of the home state of six different authors, and shares the many trials and delights of being a parent.

Bear Creek Ranch in Cathy McDavid's *Cowboy Dad* was inspired by a real guest ranch visited by the author just outside of Wickenburg, Arizona. Cathy says, "The moment we started down the long winding road leading into the ranch, I felt as if I'd stepped into a storybook." And so begins this touching story of a widowed cowboy who, much to his surprise, learns to love again.

There are five other books in the series. We hope you didn't miss Tina Leonard's *Texas Lullaby* (June 08) or *Smoky Mountain Reunion* by Lynnette Kent (July 08). And next month watch for Tanya Michaels' *A Dad for Her Twins*. Set in steamy Atlanta, this wonderful story is about second chances, doing what's right for your kids—and what's right for you. Watch for other books by authors Margot Early and Laura Marie Altom.

We hope these romantic stories inspire you to celebrate where you live—because any place you raise a child is home.

Wishing you happy reading,

Kathleen Scheibling
Senior Editor
Harlequin American Romance

Cowboy Dad
Cathy McDavid

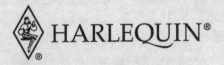

TORONTO • NEW YORK • LONDON
AMSTERDAM • PARIS • SYDNEY • HAMBURG
STOCKHOLM • ATHENS • TOKYO • MILAN • MADRID
PRAGUE • WARSAW • BUDAPEST • AUCKLAND

ISBN-13: 978-0-373-75225-6
ISBN-10:   0-373-75225-3

COWBOY DAD

ABOUT THE AUTHOR

For the past eleven years Cathy McDavid has been juggling a family, a job and writing, and has been doing pretty well at it except for the cooking and housecleaning part. Mother of boy and girl teenaged twins, she manages the near impossible by working every day with her husband of twenty years at their commercial construction company. They survive by not bringing work home and not bringing home to the office. A mutual love of all things Western also helps. Horses and ranch animals have been a part of Cathy's life since she moved to Arizona as a child and asked her mother for riding lessons. She can hardly remember a time when she couldn't walk outside and pet a soft, velvety nose (or beak, or snout) whenever the mood struck. You can visit her Web site at www.cathymcdavid.com.

Books by Cathy McDavid

HARLEQUIN AMERICAN ROMANCE

1168—HIS ONLY WIFE
1197—THE FAMILY PLAN

To Paula Eykelhof,
who saw something in that first Harlequin American
proposal and helped launch me
on the career of my dreams, and to
Kathleen Scheibling, a remarkably skilled editor
with an extraordinary eye who has
guided me through four books thus far
and I hope many more to come.

Chapter One

Natalie Forrester stood on the sweeping front porch and watched the old truck rumble down the long road, its tires kicking up a cloud of brown dust. The truck pulled a dilapidated horse trailer that rattled and banged as if it might fall apart with each pothole it hit.

As manager of guest services at Bear Creek Ranch, Natalie considered herself quite adept at determining a visitor's purpose based on the vehicle they drove. This fellow, in his seen-better-days pickup, was either a local from nearby Payson or a cowboy looking for work. Since she didn't recognize the vehicle, cowboy got her vote. Her hunch grew stronger when the driver continued through the ranch in the direction of the barn and corrals.

Whoever he was, he'd be disappointed when he met Natalie's father, head of the resort's guest amenities. Bear Creek Ranch was fully staffed for the upcoming season, scheduled to begin in a mere ten days.

And speaking of the upcoming season, Natalie had a lot of work ahead of her. Break time was over. Her feet, however, refused to heed her brain's command to turn around and march inside. The weather was unusually warm for February, the afternoon particularly balmy. According to the thermometer hanging by the front door of the main lodge, the temperature hovered in the mid-sixties. Quite nice, even for the southern edge of Arizona's rim country, which enjoyed considerably milder winters than its northern counterpart.

Natalie leaned her shoulder against a column built from a tree that had been harvested in the nearby woods about the time President John F. Kennedy took office. The wood, once rough and unfinished, had been worn smooth through the decades by thousands of shoulders belonging to the guests of Bear Creek Ranch.

She never tired of the view from the front porch. Majestic pines towered toward wispy clouds floating in a sky so blue no artist could truly capture the vibrant hue. Behind the trees, the nearby Mazatzal Mountains rose, their stair-step peaks covered in snow much of the year. Bear Creek, the ranch's namesake, could be easily reached by foot from any of the resort's thirty-three cabins. Clear and clean, the creek teemed with trout and was a favorite with guests wanting to drop a line and test their luck.

Natalie had been born on Bear Creek Ranch, in the same cabin her parents occupied today. Like her younger sister, Sabrina, she'd grown up on the ranch. Unlike Sabrina, Natalie stayed on after reaching adulthood, learning the hospitality business from the ground up.

She wasn't related to the Tuckers, the family who owned the ranch and had since it was constructed back when the railroad still made a stop at the old Bear Creek Station. But she and her parents were treated like family in many ways, and her loyalty to the Tuckers ran deep.

The front screen door banged open, rousing Natalie from her woolgathering. Alice Gilbert, the ranch's office manager and Jake Tucker's personal assistant, popped her head out the door.

"I think Shiloh's awake." She wore the expression of a person who had no experience with babies and wasn't interested in acquiring any.

"Thanks."

Pushing off the column, Natalie hurried inside. Her shoes clicked softly on the highly polished hardwood floors as she crossed the lobby toward the front desk. Alice had already disappeared into her small office, which was situated right next to Jake Tucker's larger one.

Natalie didn't have the luxury of a private office. Her position required she be available to guests whenever she was on duty and sometimes when she wasn't. Since she stood—or walked or ran if necessary—more often than she sat while working, the compact computer station tucked behind the reception desk suited her needs just fine.

It was the supply room next to her computer station that Natalie entered, listening intently. No crying. Maybe Alice had been wrong. Tiptoeing, Natalie made her way to the portable crib in the center of the floor. A Mother Goose night-light provided just enough illumination for her to make out the tiny baby stirring in the crib.

Shiloh.

As always, Natalie's heart melted at the sight of her beautiful three-month-old daughter. How did she ever get so lucky? What had been a scary unplanned pregnancy turned into the greatest joy of her life. Not a day passed that Natalie didn't thank her lucky stars.

"Hey there, sweetie pie." She bent and reached into the crib. Lifting Shiloh, she put the baby to her shoulder, kissing a crown of feather-soft hair as she did. "You hungry?"

In response, Shiloh wiggled and mewed and made sucking noises with her tiny mouth.

"Let's go, then."

Natalie left the room and headed toward Jake Tucker's office. Her boss had given her permission to use his office when he wasn't there to nurse Shiloh in privacy. Alice didn't much care for the arrangement but she had no say in the matter. Jake had insisted.

Sitting in the overstuffed leather chair behind Jake's desk, she swiveled to face the window. Shiloh was a good baby in most ways, a blessing considering her unusual day-care circumstances. Natalie nursed the baby and contemplated the changes she'd need to make soon.

The Tuckers had been generous to her since Shiloh's birth. They'd given her six weeks' maternity leave, with pay, and then allowed her to use the storage room as a makeshift nursery after she returned to work. Natalie's mother, who'd retired from Natalie's job two years ago, watched the baby for a couple hours in the morning. Jake's oldest daughter helped out when she got home from school.

It was those hours in between that were the problem. Natalie couldn't keep Shiloh with her during the day when the ranch reopened for the new season. Hiring a part-time nanny made the most sense, but finding a trusted candidate she could afford on her modest budget wouldn't be easy.

Balancing Shiloh in her lap, Natalie rubbed the baby's back and waited for a burp. When Shiloh showed no more interest in nursing, Natalie buttoned her blouse. Not an easy task with a baby in her lap. She started when the door unexpectedly opened, hurrying to smooth her disarrayed clothing. Shiloh gave a fussy cry in response.

"Just a second," Natalie said, feeling her cheeks flush. Although she had permission to be there, she was nonetheless embarrassed. She stood up and turned around, Shiloh cradled in her arms, an apology on the tip of her tongue.

Only it wasn't Jake Tucker who stood just inside the doorway. This man was a complete stranger.

"May I help you?" Her voice squeaked slightly.

"Sorry to disturb you, ma'am." He removed his battered cowboy hat. "The lady out front didn't tell me anyone was in here."

"Not your fault." Natalie mustered her best be-nice-to-the-guests smile. Alice's oversight may or may not have been intentional. No point getting upset about it.

"The fellow down at the stables told me to wait here for Tucker."

Two things about the man's statement struck Natalie as odd. First was the fact her father sent the cowboy to the main lodge.

Even if they were looking to hire another hand, her father didn't need Jake's approval for that.

Second, no one Natalie knew or had ever met referred to Jacob Tucker by his last name alone. Family and close friends called him Jake. Everyone else, including Natalie except when they were in private, called him *Mr.* Tucker.

"Did Alice phone him for you?"

"If that's the lady out front, I believe she did. Said he'd be right along."

He smiled at Natalie then, and she was surprised to find herself thinking what an attractive man he was. Dark brown eyes and even darker hair hinted at a Hispanic heritage. His shoulders were wide but proportionate to his height and well muscled. This cowboy, in his faded jeans and worn-at-the-elbows work shirt, was accustomed to hard physical labor. It was a look he carried well.

"All right then." Natalie took a step toward the door, intending to leave. Her curiosity was definitely piqued, but this man's meeting with Jake was none of her business.

"Your baby's very pretty."

His words stopped her. She received many compliments on Shiloh, but rarely from men and never from men who were strangers.

"Thank you."

His smile warmed, and Natalie relaxed. She met all types of people in her line of work. Though appearances could be deceiving, she was a quick and fairly accurate judge of character. This cowboy didn't strike her as a troublemaker or a creep. If anything, she sensed the opposite in him. There was a quiet sadness underlying his pleasant manner. Subtle, but definitely there.

"Her father must be very proud of her," he said.

"I wouldn't know." Her response came unexpectedly. She didn't reveal much to anyone about Shiloh's absent father, preferring to dodge questions rather than reply.

"His loss," the man said simply.

"Yes, it is," Natalie said and automatically held a dozy Shiloh closer. "I'd best go."

He inclined his head. "Maybe I'll see you around the ranch."

There was nothing flirtatious about his statement, but Natalie still kept her tone professional. "If you're staying, that's likely."

"I'm staying."

"You sound very sure."

"It's taken me two years to get here. And now that I am, I'm not leaving. For any reason," he added.

"I see." Another odd comment, Natalie mused. But then everything about this man and his visit was out of the ordinary…and interesting, she silently admitted.

In the ten months since Shiloh's father left—with the same abruptness he'd come into her life—Natalie avoided encounters with the opposite sex. So why pick today to lower her guard? And with someone she'd met in a less than comfortable situation only moments before?

Hurried footsteps echoed in the lobby.

"Mr. Tucker's here."

The man gave an unconcerned shrug and if she wasn't mistaken, his sad eyes twinkled with the barest hint of amusement.

In the next instant, Jake burst through the door. A fine sheen of perspiration covered his forehead, and a lock of hair hung limply over his brow. Natalie couldn't help staring at her boss's uncustomary disheveled state.

"Oh." He appeared taken aback to find her in his office. "You two have met."

"Not exactly," Natalie stammered.

"I inadvertently walked in on her," the man offered. "We haven't been officially introduced yet."

He was smiling again, and Natalie flushed anew. Had he come into the office a minute sooner, he'd have caught her nursing Shiloh.

Jake combed fingers through his hair, restoring it to a semblance of its normal tidiness. "Natalie Forrester is our manager of guest services." He indicated the man with a curt nod and a throat clearing. "And this is Aaron Reyes."

Natalie forced her slack-jawed mouth to close. "How do you do," she murmured when her wits returned.

"He was my sister's husband," Jake clarified.

He needn't have bothered—Natalie knew the name. She'd heard it shouted, whispered, trashed and taken in vain plenty often during the last few years. But never once uttered with warmth or affection.

"I'll leave you two alone," she said and made a beeline for the door. Shiloh protested the bumpy ride with a soft cry.

"It was nice meeting you, ma'am," he called after her.

"Same here."

"Don't go far," Jake said before Natalie closed the door. "I'll need you to show Reyes here to his quarters."

"Yes, sir."

So, he *was* staying. For eight weeks if he abided by the terms of the Tucker Family Trust.

"Well, I'll be damned," Natalie muttered to herself. Aaron Reyes, husband of the late Hailey Tucker, had come at long last to Bear Creek Ranch to claim his inheritance.

Of all the men she could take notice of, it had to be the one her boss despised with every breath he drew.

"If there was any way I could legally kick your ass off this place, I would."

"I understand."

Aaron didn't take offense at Jake's outburst. His former brother-in-law had a right to be angry at him for waiting until practically the last day to exercise his right to a share of the Tucker Family Trust. Jake didn't, however, have any cause to be mad at Aaron for marrying Hailey. He'd loved his wife and treated her well. They'd been happy together for six months, would have been happy together for the rest of their lives if fate hadn't intervened.

Whether it was their marriage or Aaron's claim to his inheritance that infuriated Jake was irrelevant. Aaron had made an enemy the day he eloped with Jake's younger sister—more than one enemy if Jake wielded the kind of power Hailey always said he did.

"You'll receive no preferential treatment," Jake continued through tightly clenched teeth.

"I don't expect any."

The two men squared off across an oversize oak desk, Jake sat behind it, Aaron in front of it.

"Everyone here works hard. Sunup to sundown. Longer if necessary."

"My kind of hours."

Jake snorted, then snatched a paper off his desk as if he just that second realized something needed his attention.

Aaron waited. He could play the game, had been prepared to do just that. For the longest time after Hailey died he'd had nothing to do with the Tuckers or the inheritance she'd left him, despite it being her wish he get to know her family and the ranch her grandparents founded.

A month ago, as the deadline for him to act approached, Aaron changed his mind. He was glad he did. Sparring with Jake made him feel truly alive for the first time since he'd knelt in that arena, an unconscious Hailey in his arms. She never woke up. The fall, a freak riding accident, had crushed her skull beyond repair. She died four hours later in a hospital bed, surrounded by people who loved her—and who disliked each other intensely.

"Breakfast is at 6:00 a.m. sharp. Lunch at noon." Jake set his paper aside. "You'll eat with the staff, not the guests."

"Beats chowing on a can of refried beans in the back of my pickup."

Jake gave a noncommittal grunt. "Dinner at six. Then you'll be *required* to eat with the guests."

"Really?" Aaron raised an eyebrow.

"Ranch policy. Not my personal one. The guests enjoy mingling with the hands."

"And that's what I'll be doing while I'm here? Ranch hand?"

"Report to Gary Forrester in the morning. Before breakfast," Jake emphasized.

"The man who directed me here?"

"Yes. He'll decide your job."

If Jake were in charge of assigning jobs, Aaron thought wryly, he'd probably pick head manure shoveler.

"Is Gary Forrester any relation to Natalie Forrester?"

"Her father. He oversees our riding stock, the stables and the wranglers, among other things."

Aaron thought of the young woman he'd met earlier in Jake's office. She'd done her best to downplay her natural prettiness. No makeup to accent intelligent blue eyes. She wore a stretchy headband that only half tamed a mop of wild blond curls, and baggy jeans and sweater that did little to hide a very female shape beneath.

He wasn't interested in complicating his life with romantic entanglements but if he ever changed his mind, Natalie Forrester would be a woman worth tangling with.

"Do I talk to Ms. Forrester about paying for my room and board?"

"You don't pay." Jake ground the teeth he'd been previously clenching. "Members of the trust receive meals and lodging as part of the deal."

Another man might have grabbed Aaron by the shirt collar the second he spotted him in the lobby and tossed him out on his rear. Not Jake Tucker. Settling disputes through a show of physical force wasn't his style. Whatever efforts he employed to rid the ranch of Aaron—and he would employ them, Aaron was sure of it—were bound to be less direct, more subtle and cast no blame on him.

He'd tried the legal route soon after Hailey's death. The courts sided with Aaron, holding up the terms of Hailey's will. At the time, he hadn't cared. He'd wished, in fact, the judge had ruled against him.

But a month ago, Aaron found a use for the income from his inheritance and a way to bring meaning to Hailey's otherwise purposeless death.

His former brother-in-law probably wouldn't see it that way.

But how Aaron spent the money from his share of the trust was his concern and his concern alone. Now, he just needed to keep that income rolling in. Which was what brought him to Bear Creek Ranch in the first place a mere two days before he would have forfeited his voting rights in the trust.

The deal, as Jake called it, wasn't complicated. Neither was it easy. Members of the Tucker Family Trust who didn't already live on the ranch were required to stay for a minimum of eight weeks every year and work alongside the regular staff. It was the founding members' intention that those who belonged to the trust and were responsible for making decisions affecting the ranch have a firsthand understanding of its operation.

Aaron spent the past few weeks making the necessary arrangements to enable him to take some time off. He hadn't advised Jake of his plans, preferring to surprise him. Aaron needed every advantage at his disposal if he were to last the full eight weeks.

"Staff housing isn't like guest cabins," Jake said, "and is located on another part of the ranch. You'll share your quarters with three or four other employees, depending on what's available."

"Okay." Aaron was no stranger to cohabitating with a bunch of guys. Ten years of traveling the professional rodeo circuit and living hand to mouth had taught him to make do with what was available. If that included sleeping on a hotel-room floor or in the back of his pickup, so be it.

"Natalie will show you around."

"I'm looking forward to it." Aaron meant nothing by his remark, but the unfriendly glare Jake shot him made him feel like a lecherous old man.

"Stay away from her," he snarled.

"Hey, take it easy."

"I don't give a damn about the conditions of the trust. You touch Natalie, you hurt her, and I personally guarantee you'll never sit a bronc the same way again. Your rodeo career will be over."

Not much of a threat. Aaron quit rodeoing right after Hailey died. Apparently, Jake didn't know, and Aaron didn't bother to enlighten him.

"Look, I'm not interested in her." Since what Aaron said was the truth, he saw no reason to engage Jake in an argument. They would have enough problems getting along without adding to them.

"Remember what I said." Jake leveled a finger at him.

Protective. He'd been like that with Hailey, too. Or, was it controlling?

Considering the intensity of his warning, Aaron thought his former brother-in-law might assume the duty of showing him to his quarters. Instead, the phone on the desk rang, and he dismissed Aaron with a brusque "That's all for now."

Natalie was waiting for him outside the office. More accurately, she was seated at a computer and looked up expectantly when he emerged.

Aaron felt a small something when their gazes connected…and held. Not exactly a spark. More of a brief flicker. It was hard to tell. His sensors were pretty rusty.

Maybe Jake had been right to warn him away from Natalie after all.

If he wanted to stay, wanted to make this plan of his work, he'd be wise to heed that warning.

Chapter Two

"We're fully staffed. The only bunkhouse with an empty bed in it right now is fourteen." Natalie talked as she maneuvered the electric golf cart with practiced ease.

Aaron gritted his teeth and held on to the seat edge as they took yet another sharp turn on an uneven, tree-lined dirt road that was more of a trail than anything else. "Fourteen's my lucky number."

She chuckled. "You say that now."

"Why are you laughing?" He took his eyes off the road long enough to cast her a suspicious glance. "What's wrong with the bunkhouse?"

"Nothing." Her grin widened. "It's your bunkmates."

"I'll manage. I've shared quarters with some real winners in the past. It kind of comes with the territory."

"Good. You'll have the necessary experience to draw on." She turned her wide and, he admitted, dazzling grin on him.

It was contagious, and Aaron couldn't resist responding. He was suddenly looking forward to meeting his bunkmates. Life, he realized, had become mundane. Today was the most enjoyment he'd had in he couldn't remember when.

Natalie had left her baby back at the lodge in the care of a young teenage girl named Briana. Jake's oldest and, Aaron supposed, his niece by marriage. She'd heard about him—nothing good, based on the wary once-over she gave him. He liked her anyway because she obviously adored Natalie's baby and couldn't wait to swing the infant up in her arms.

"Here we are." Natalie brought the golf cart to a stop in front of a simple, yet well-maintained, bunkhouse. It was the third in a sizable row of bunkhouses, all alike except for the angle at which they were tucked into the hill.

Aaron climbed out of the golf cart and retrieved his duffel bag from the back. He and Natalie had stopped first at the stables before coming here. Aaron checked on his horse, Dollar, and then grabbed his stuff. He traveled light. Another holdover from his former career.

"A laptop?" Natalie asked, eyeing the black computer case he slung over his shoulder.

He purposely didn't tell her why he'd brought it. "Is there a phone line in the bunkhouse?"

"No. But the ranch has a wireless connection in the main lodge. It's for the convenience of our guests, but the staff use it, too."

"Thanks."

She kept staring at the laptop, though she asked no more questions about it. "The dining hall is to the east of the main lodge. The building with the picnic tables out front and the big outdoor fireplace. You have about an hour and a half before dinner."

What had been a four-minute golf-cart ride would be a fifteen-minute walk. Aaron checked his watch. He had plenty of time to shower and clean up before meeting his coworkers at dinner. Or, was that employees since he technically owned one-eighth of the ranch?

Better to come off as a coworker, he decided, if he wished to fit in and make friends with the staff. Aaron had a reason to be here, and it wasn't to show anyone who was boss. He'd leave that to Jake.

"See you at dinner," Natalie said and drove off.

Something else for Aaron to look forward to, he thought, watching her putt-putt down the road.

Only after she disappeared from sight did he turn and walk up the steep path to the bunkhouse. At the door, he set down his duffel bag and tried the knob. The hinges squeaked when he opened the unlocked door, announcing his arrival.

"Anyone home?"

No one answered so he went inside.

The bunkhouse was small, yet comfortable. A two-person breakfast bar separated the galley kitchen from the living room. Three rooms led off a short hallway; two bedrooms and a bathroom the size of a large closet. Furniture was sparse. Each bedroom contained a set of twin beds and a single dresser.

Both rooms were occupied, as evidenced by shoes left in the middle of the floor and toiletries on the dresser tops. Aaron opted to wait and see which bed was available before stowing his things. Taking some clean clothes from his duffel bag, he hit the shower. He met two of his bunkmates when he finished a short time later.

"Hey," a guy with a scruffy goatee greeted him from the kitchen. He was wearing a tan shirt and matching pants. "How's it going?"

He appeared neither surprised nor annoyed to find a stranger using his bathroom. The same could be said for the guy on the couch, who wore an identical uniform and was stretched out with his feet propped up on a thrift-store-style coffee table, listening to his iPod.

"Want one?" The guy in the kitchen held up a beer.

"No, thanks."

"Can't drink alcohol anywhere but inside your bunkhouse," the guy told Aaron before tipping back his longneck bottle and taking a lengthy pull. "They're real strict about that. If a guest sees you drinking, you'll be fired on the spot."

"I'll keep that in mind." Aaron unzipped his duffel bag and removed a plastic sack. He added dirty clothes to his growing pile. "Is there a laundry around here?"

"Behind the dining hall." The guy hitched his chin as if the laundry were right across the road rather than a good mile up it. "By the way, I'm Randy. That there is Skunk."

"Skunk?"

Randy shook his head. "Don't ask. You'll just make him mad."

If Skunk knew they were talking about him he gave no indication. Head resting on the back of the couch, he listened to his iPod with closed eyes. He might have been napping except for the beer he raised to his lips every other minute like clockwork.

"I'm Aaron."

"Nice to meet you." Randy toasted him. "Where you from?"

"Laveen, originally," he answered, naming the small rural community southeast of Phoenix where he was born and raised. "I've been traveling a lot since I graduated high school."

"Yeah, haven't we all."

"Which bed is mine?" Aaron didn't suppose either of these two would make a bad roommate. Randy appeared agreeable enough and Skunk was quiet.

A slow smile spread across Randy's face. "Me and Skunk got the room to the right."

"Who's in the bedroom to the left?"

Randy's smile expanded until it stretched from ear to ear. "Terrence." He said the name with both reverence and amusement.

Aaron got the distinct impression he was the brunt of some joke only Randy was in on. He decided to go along with it for now. Nothing wrong with a little sport among friends.

"What do you and Skunk do on the ranch?" he asked.

"Skunk's with maintenance, and I'm with groundskeeping. He keeps the rental ATVs running for the guests. I pick up their litter." Randy took another swig of his beer. "It's not such a bad living I reckon. What about you?"

"Ranch hand, I think. I'm supposed to report to Gary Forrester in the morning."

"You'll be working with Terrence then." Randy's smile became ridiculously large.

Aaron began to suspect he was in for a real treat when he

met this Terrence, and not a good one. He was just getting the rundown on the community tipping pool when a heavy thumping sounded from the porch.

Randy shot out from behind the breakfast bar. "Terrence is home."

Skunk opened his eyes and removed his headphones, letting them fall onto his lap.

Whoever this Terrence was, he commanded a lot of attention.

The door flew open. A tall, broad, dark figure stopped and stood, filling every inch of the open space. Arms ripped with muscles extended from a sleeveless work shirt. Boots—size thirteen at least—stepped over the threshold and came down with a hard clunk on the bare floor, the spurs jangling. A rattlesnake tattoo wound around a thick, corded neck.

Aaron swallowed, admittedly intimidated. He'd met cowboys who looked more like homeboys, but never a cow*girl*.

"Hi, Terrence," Randy chirped. "Meet your new roomie."

She stared at Randy as if she might eat him alive for breakfast. "My name ain't Terrence. It's Teresa." She enunciated each syllable while pointing a finger at him with the same aggression some people raised a fist. "And you morons better start calling me that."

"It's really nice to meet you, Teresa." Aaron considered shaking her hand but decided she might inadvertently crush his fingers.

"I don't room with no one." She glared at him. "That was the agreement when I took this job."

"Guess the agreement's changed." Randy burst into laughter. So did Skunk. They both shut up when Teresa fixed her glare on them.

"We'll just see what Natalie has to say about this."

"Why don't I sleep on the couch," Aaron suggested.

"Good idea." Teresa removed her hat and sailed it across the room. It landed on the coffee table, inches from Skunk's feet. She wiped her damp forehead and patted her many rows of tight braids, woven with beads of all colors. "I'm taking a shower. Anyone who steps foot in the bathroom is a dead man."

No one so much as blinked.

"She seems personable," Aaron said when she'd gone into the bathroom and slammed the door shut behind her.

When Randy and Skunk broke into more laughter, Aaron joined them. His good mood lasted up until dinner when everyone in the dining hall turned to stare when he and his bunkmates walked in.

"What gives?" Randy asked, checking out all the gawking faces.

"There's something I didn't mention," Aaron said, wondering if their friendly treatment of him would change after he told them who he really was.

"So, WHAT'S HE LIKE?" Natalie's mother, Deana, asked in a whisper that somehow managed to carry over the noisy din of the crowded dining hall.

There were twenty-nine employees currently on the Bear Creek Ranch payroll. By Natalie's estimation, each and every one of them was there, eating dinner and staying long after they'd finished for another look at Aaron Reyes. Her mother was no exception, sneaking less than discreet glances his way every few seconds.

"Seems pleasant enough," her father said. He was one of the only people there more concerned with eating his apple pie than Aaron Reyes's unexpected appearance on the ranch.

"Very pleasant," Natalie concurred, shaking a rattle in front of Shiloh's face.

She'd put the baby in a carrier, one that doubled as a car seat, and secured it on the chair beside her. Shiloh had been restless most of the dinner and was getting fussier by the minute. Probably a reaction to the nervous energy abounding in the room, so different from the usual staff meals where everyone joked and told stories and decompressed after a hard day of work.

Meals were served family style at the ranch. Everyone dined at long tables holding twelve to fourteen people, and enjoyed simple, country fare. After the start of the new season, the staff, with the exception of the ranch hands and trail guides, would take their meals an hour earlier than the guests and eat either in the kitchen or outside beneath the ramada. Until then, they all ate together in the dining hall.

"Pleasant? That's all you have to say?" Deana threw Aaron Reyes another sidelong glance.

"Polite," Natalie added.

"Right sociable," her father said.

"Likes kids."

"Likes kids?" Deana looked inquisitively at Natalie. "How do you know that?"

"I don't." Natalie backpedaled. "Just a feeling." Because he'd complimented Shiloh? Not much to go on, really. "What I mean is he doesn't dislike kids." That remark earned her an eye roll from her mother. *Shut up,* she told herself, *while you can still save face.*

Natalie's father came to her rescue. "He knows a lot about horses."

"Well, he should," Deana said with a huff. "He was national bronc-riding champion for three straight years. Saddle and bareback."

Only half listening, Natalie put the rattle in Shiloh's pudgy hand. The baby immediately thrust the rattle into her mouth and began gnawing on it, freeing Natalie to drink her coffee and eat her pie.

"He's a fine-looking man."

Natalie hoped her lack of response would bring about a change of topic. Her efforts were in vain.

"I'll say. He's hot," Alice Gilbert added. She sat directly across from Natalie and had been watching Aaron along with her mother. "Did you see him in those magazine ads? Whew! Made me want to buy vet supplies and I don't even own a horse."

"And what about that cable-TV show he was on for a while?" Deana elbowed Natalie's father. "You used to watch it."

"Rodeo Week in Review," he mumbled.

"That's it." Deana quit trying to be subtle and openly studied Aaron. "No one could blame Hailey falling for him. How much younger than her was he?" She answered her own question before someone else could. "Four years, right? No, five. Which, of course, is no big deal these days."

Natalie remembered the age difference really bothering Jake. But then, everything about his little sister's marriage bothered him.

"How much money do you think he has?"

"Mom!"

"Did you see that silver belt buckle he's wearing? The thing has to be worth a couple thousand dollars. I bet he has a whole drawer full of them."

"His truck isn't worth much more than that belt buckle," Natalie's father commented. "Whatever money he made rodeoing must be spent."

"If he ever made any money at it to begin with," Alice added with a knowing look. "I heard Jake say once that Aaron Reyes only married his sister for her money and the family connection."

Natalie had her doubts. While certainly comfortable, the Tuckers weren't as rich as they looked. And an ex-national rodeo champion who regularly appeared in magazine ads and on television wasn't someone who needed the clout of the Tucker name. In her opinion, her boss had been looking for reasons to dislike Aaron.

"Maybe he blew all his money," Deana offered.

"Or lost it on bad investments," Alice suggested.

"Stop it, all of you." Natalie frowned at her tablemates. Though she secretly agreed with her father's assessment of Aaron's financial situation, she refused to gossip about him. "You're as bad as everyone else here."

Deana rushed to their defense. "Naturally, we're curious. Who wouldn't be?"

"Aren't you the least bit curious, too?" her father asked. A slight smile pulled at the corners of his mouth.

Natalie tried to muster up some annoyance and failed. He knew her too well, better even than her mother and sister. "A little," she admitted out loud. *A lot,* she admitted to herself. "But I won't gossip about him."

She herself had been the subject of countless dinner-table discussions when her flash-in-the-pan romance with Shiloh's father ended.

Natalie met Shiloh's father at the Payson rodeo last year when Jake's cousin, Carolina, coerced her into going. For all her twenty-seven years, Natalie didn't have much experience with men. Fraternizing with the guests was strictly prohibited. Guests were pretty much the only men Natalie met. As a result, she didn't date much. Okay, hardly at all.

Like Aaron Reyes, Shiloh's father made his living as a professional rodeo rider, though he wasn't nearly as successful. He'd swept Natalie off her feet with his easy charm and heart-stopping sexy smile. She succumbed quickly, and when he didn't leave right away for the next rodeo, she started hoping he'd stay on and that maybe her father would give him a job on the ranch.

The positive home-pregnancy test panicked him. It had panicked her, too. He might have done the right thing eventually, given the time and the chance. Married her, stayed on the ranch, paid monthly child support. But Natalie sent him packing the second she realized how much he didn't want a child. She'd justified her actions, saying she deserved more than an irresponsible drifter for a husband and that Shiloh deserved a father who wanted her. But there were nights when she lay in bed awake, wondering if she'd been wrong to act so hastily.

Aaron Reyes reminded her too much of Shiloh's father. No matter how interesting he might be, how "fine-looking" he was, how pleasant he seemed, Natalie had dated her last rodeo rider. More importantly, her boss didn't like Aaron, and she refused to go against the Tuckers. Not voluntarily.

Shiloh began crying. Natalie unbuckled the straps holding her daughter in the carrier and lifted her out, automatically checking her diaper. It was dry. A few soothing words whispered in her ear helped to settle her.

"He can't be that broke." Deana wasn't ready to abandon the topic of Aaron Reyes. "Not with the money he gets from the family trust."

"Depends on annual profits," Alice said. "We had a few lean years there, though things are picking up."

Based on advance bookings, the ranch was in for the busiest season they'd had in a long while.

"And a lot of Jake Tucker's wealth comes from his business investments outside of the ranch." Her father gave her mother a very pointed stare.

"True." Deana had the decency to look chagrined.

When she'd retired from Natalie's job, it was to pursue a longtime dream of owning and running her own business. With Jake Tucker's financial backing, she and Millie Sweetwater, Jake's aunt, opened an antique shop in Payson that was so far operating in the black and showed promise of really taking off. Jake, Natalie knew, was satisfied with the return on his investment.

Yet one more reason for Natalie to steer clear of Aaron Reyes. It was unlikely Jake would withdraw his support of the business because of his aunt. But if he did, Natalie's mother would suffer. Possibly lose the business. Jake and his aunt could withstand the financial hit. Not Deana.

Shiloh finally had enough and was now crying in earnest.

"I think this is my cue to go home." Natalie returned Shiloh to the carrier and refastened the straps, then stood. "I'll see you all in the morning." She went around the table to the other side and gave each of her parents a kiss on the cheek.

"Night, baby girl." Deana reached out and tickled Shiloh's

sock-covered foot. "I hope she doesn't keep you up all hours of the night."

"She'll be fine once we get home." Shiloh usually went to sleep quickly and often as not, didn't wake up until morning. "I might walk around a bit first. Fresh air makes her sleepy."

"You sure? It's getting cold out there."

Natalie tucked a blanket around the baby. "We won't be long."

She noticed Aaron still sitting and chatting as she wove between the tables and headed toward the kitchen. Apparently, he'd yet to grow weary of hearing his name on every person's lips. Good for him.

Taking a shortcut through the kitchen, she stopped at the walk-in refrigerator and grabbed a bottled water before going outside. The instant they hit the cool evening air, Shiloh stopped crying and started looking around.

The peace and quiet was a welcome relief. Natalie paused a moment to enjoy the silence before cutting across a small strip of lawn that ran between the dining hall and the main lodge. She'd driven her compact car from her bunkhouse, not wanting to take Shiloh in the golf cart.

Light spilled from a window in the laundry room behind the kitchen, catching Natalie's attention. She sighed and changed direction. This was hardly the first time she had to follow behind careless employees, shutting off lights they left on or picking up their discarded trash.

An empty bag sat atop one of the washers. Natalie looked around and when she saw nothing else amiss, switched off the light. She turned to leave…only to shop short when she came face-to-face with Aaron Reyes.

"Oh!" Her heart suddenly beat faster. "You startled me."

"Sorry. I didn't realize anyone was here." He moved aside to let her pass.

She stepped around him, carefully maneuvering Shiloh's carrier. "I'm always shutting lights off." She flicked the switch, turning the light back on.

"My fault. I'll be more careful next time."

He flashed her a smile. Not threatening or predatory or even sexy like Shiloh's father. Just nice.

Although Natalie should have left—did her long talk with herself at dinner mean nothing?—she lingered. "How are you getting on with your bunkmates?"

"Great."

"I should have warned you about Teresa."

"What? And take all the fun out of it?" He pulled wet clothes from the washer and tossed them in the dryer.

"I really didn't have any choice but to put you with them. Our employee contracts limit the number of people we can assign to a bunkhouse."

"I like sleeping on the couch."

Natalie winced. "I'm pretty sure we have a cot in one of the storage rooms. I'll check on it tomorrow."

"I'm fine," he said, pushing a button on the dryer. With a squeaky groan, the drum started spinning.

"You say that now. But after eight weeks—"

"I'll still be fine. Really."

A moment passed with neither of them moving. Even Shiloh quieted, her little arms no longer wiggling.

Natalie broke the silence. "Can I at least give you a ride to your bunkhouse?"

"No, thanks. I'll walk back with my new roomies after my clothes are dry."

"Okay."

Her estimation of Aaron rose another notch. No one would think much of her giving one of the owners a ride. They would think a whole lot more of that owner if he walked.

Natalie took a step toward the door. There really was no reason to stay. So why didn't she leave? "You going back to the dining hall?"

Aaron leaned a hip on the washing machine. "In a few minutes. I have some calls to make."

Her eyes automatically went to the cell phone clipped to his belt. "You can't get a signal everywhere on the ranch. It's best near the main lodge and only when the weather's not overcast."

His expression warmed. "I'll keep that in mind."

Natalie wanted to bite her tongue. The line she delivered ten times a day to guests had sounded like an invitation to walk with her. It was all the incentive she needed to finally get a move on.

"Good night, then."

"See you tomorrow."

Stepping outside, she decided it would be for the best if she avoided Aaron as much as possible in the coming weeks. Technically, she worked for him, and it was her duty, her responsibility, to be helpful. But helpful didn't include chitchatting in the laundry room. The last thing she wanted was for him to get the wrong idea.

Leaving him behind, she backtracked the way she'd come, her gaze focused on the uneven ground ahead. A shadow entered her line of vision. For the second time that night, she stopped short just before colliding with someone. Only this someone was her boss. Jake Tucker.

She didn't need to see his face to know he wasn't happy.

Chapter Three

Natalie skipped her usual sit-down breakfast the next morning. She had a hundred and one things to do and only two hours of uninterrupted work time while her mother watched Shiloh. After that, Deana would leave for the antique shop in Payson, an easy twenty-minute drive south on the highway.

Entering the dining hall, Natalie headed straight for the coffee station and filled her jumbo travel mug. On her way to the kitchen, she stopped by one of the tables and grabbed an English muffin, wrapping it in a napkin.

"Morning, honey," her father called from the opposite table.

"Hey, Dad."

Any other day, Natalie would have rushed over to give her father a quick hug or peck on the cheek. But this morning, he sat with Aaron Reyes, and they looked rather chummy with their heads bent, going over papers and maps and handwritten lists.

It wasn't just their obvious involvement in whatever they were discussing that gave Natalie pause. Jake's warning from the previous night still rang in her ears. He hadn't told her not to talk to Aaron ever again, but he didn't have to. She'd worked for Jake in some capacity since she was fourteen and long ago learned to read between his spoken lines.

"Gotta run." She waved a hand at her father and smiled brightly, hoping neither he nor Aaron realized they were being snubbed. "See you later." Sipping her coffee, she hurried toward the kitchen.

Natalie had her own list to go over with Olivia Barraza, supervisor of the kitchen crew and indisputable queen of her domain.

"Buenos días, chiquita," she said to Natalie upon seeing her come into the kitchen. Though it had been a good many years since Natalie was a *little girl,* Olivia still used the endearment.

When Natalie took over her mother's position, she'd worried that some of the staff, particularly those employees like Olivia who'd watched Natalie grow up and, on occasion, supervised her, wouldn't accept her once they were on equal footing.

In Olivia's case, Natalie's worries were for nothing. They worked well together. When they weren't on duty, Olivia treated Natalie like a beloved niece and Shiloh like one of her numerous grandchildren.

"I've got the most recent advance-booking numbers to go over with you." Natalie pulled a stool up to the counter and took a seat. Weekly menus varied, depending on the number of guests staying at the ranch. To ensure the food served was the freshest possible, orders weren't placed until the last minute.

Olivia dried her hands on a dish towel and came over to join Natalie. She was followed by one of her helpers, who, like Olivia, had been cleaning up after breakfast. The dishwasher, a young man barely into his twenties, remained at the sink, scrubbing a pot.

No sooner would the last fork be washed and dried and put away than the staff would start preparing lunch. When the new season started and there was an army of hungry guests to feed, twice the current staff would run the kitchen sixteen hours a day, operating with the precision and efficiency of a factory assembly line. Olivia tolerated nothing less.

"Before you get into that—" she settled herself onto the stool beside Natalie with a grace that belied her generous size "—there's something we want to talk to you about."

"We?"

She nodded at her helper. "Gerrie and I. Lucia and Pat, too," she said, referring to her other two helpers who weren't there.

"About what?" Natalie asked, a tad uneasy. Olivia was so rarely somber.

"Shiloh."

"Shiloh?"

"Yes." Olivia inched closer. So did Gerrie.

Natalie felt surrounded. "I don't understand."

"We know you need a babysitter and can't find one."

"That's true. But—"

"We'll do it." Olivia and Gerrie exchanged nods.

Natalie's glance went from one woman to the next. "You two?"

"We four. Lucia and Pat want to help, too."

"Don't look at me," the dishwasher said from the sink when Natalie turned in his direction. "Kids are scared of me."

With his piercings, scraggly goatee and full-sleeve tatts, Natalie believed him.

"But your days off," she sputtered, still struggling to absorb everything Olivia had said. "You'd give them up?"

"Not all of them. We would rotate." Olivia pulled a folded sheet of paper from her apron pocket and handed it to Natalie. "I've already talked to your mother and Briana. We need everyone to make this work."

Natalie scanned the paper. On it was a seven-day grid with names penciled inside the squares, including her own. Olivia had gone though a lot of work to put it together.

"I don't know what to say." Natalie's throat tightened.

"You say okay and thank you."

"I'm really touched." She tried to hand the paper back to Olivia. "But it's too much to ask of you."

"This is temporary," Olivia assured Natalie, patting her arm. "Until you make other arrangements."

"I'll pay you," Natalie insisted. "It's only fair."

"All right." Olivia conceded with a shrug.

Natalie would have refused their plan unless they'd agreed to accept payment, and Olivia knew it.

"You sure, too?" Natalie looked inquiringly at Gerrie.

"Hey, I can use the extra money."

"What about your boyfriend?"

Gerrie giggled. "Why do you think I need the extra money?"

"Only until I hire a regular nanny," Natalie reiterated over a catch in her throat.

"Of course." Olivia beamed.

Natalie drew in a breath, composed herself, then said, "Okay and thank you."

The three woman hugged. Natalie wasn't sure what she'd done to deserve such good friends. She'd have to find a way besides money to return their kindness.

For the next ten minutes, Natalie and Olivia went over the bookings and discussed food orders. Afterward, Natalie left through the dining area on her way next door to the main lodge. Her father and Aaron were gone, much to her relief. She wouldn't have to find an excuse for avoiding Aaron.

Olivia and Gerrie had reminded her of what she already knew in her heart. The employees of Bear Creek Ranch weren't just coworkers or even friends. They were family.

And Natalie would be a fool to jeopardize her place here by having anything other than a strictly professional relationship with Aaron.

THE CLINK, CLINK of a hammer against an iron anvil resounded through the crisp morning air. Seven horses stood tied to the hitching rail beside the barn entrance, their tails swishing and ears flicking. Six awaited their turn with the farrier. The seventh one belonged to Aaron.

Teresa and another ranch hand Aaron just met that morning helped the farrier. With forty head of riding stock to shoe, they had their work cut out for them.

Aaron's lone female bunkmate had yet to warm to him, though he was pretty sure he sensed a slight crumbling of her hard exterior. The couch was about as comfortable as a sack of potatoes, and too short for his six-one frame. But, sad to say, he'd slept on worse. Not, however, for eight straight weeks. He rolled his shoulders to loosen some of the knots, thinking he might take Natalie up on her offer of a cot.

She'd avoided him at breakfast, and he was surprised at the depth of his disappointment. Until she abruptly escaped into the kitchen, he hadn't known how much he was hoping she'd sit with him and her father. Did Jake talk to her? Warn her away as he had Aaron? He wouldn't put it past the man.

All the more reason for Aaron to seek her out at dinner and ask her about the cot.

Talking softly to Dollar, Aaron hefted his saddle onto the horse's back. When he pulled the girth tight, Dollar snaked his big head around and gave him *the look*.

"Sorry, boy." He let the girth out. "Didn't realize you'd put on a few pounds around the middle."

The horse turned back to the fence, clearly insulted.

"Hey, you're not the only one." Aaron patted the front of his denim jacket. "Truth is, we're both out of shape."

He rode as often as he could. These days, "often" amounted to once, sometimes twice, a week. There'd been a time when he rode daily. When they weren't rodeoing, Aaron and Dollar competed in team penning events—mostly for fun and only on a local level. That was how he'd met Hailey, when he congratulated her on beating the pants off him. He'd never been so happy to lose.

She was an experienced rider and careful. Not one to take unnecessary risks. Which was why her accident was so difficult to accept.

The mere click of a photographer's camera was to blame. Her horse bolted at the insignificant sound just as they were exiting the arena after a successful run and an unprepared Hailey went flying. She bounced off the fence like a discarded rag doll and landed directly under the mare's thrashing hooves. Two dozen people instantly poured from the sidelines but were too late to drag her to safety.

Aaron would never forget the horror on the photographer's face.

Ironically, the mare had been Hailey's favorite. They'd had hundreds of photos taken of them, appeared in dozens of publications. Why that particular day the mare spooked at something so familiar was a question Aaron had spent almost two years asking himself. He stopped only when he decided to come to Bear Creek Ranch and make Hailey's death count for something.

"Be right back, boy." Aaron patted Dollar's neck and, leaving the girth undone, strolled to the side of the barn. He kept a toolbox in the storage compartment of his trailer.

"Need something?" Gary hollered to him from the barn aisle. He carried a fifty-pound saddle over one arm with the same ease most people carried a sack of groceries.

"Leather punch. Seems my horse has been cheating on his diet again."

"There's one in there if you want." Gary hitched his chin in the direction of the tack room.

"Appreciate it." When Aaron passed Gary, he noted the worn but superior-crafted saddle. Natalie's father evidently didn't spend all his days taking novice riders on trail rides through easy terrain.

"You do much endurance riding?" Aaron asked.

"Not like I used to." Gary stopped, assessed Aaron with a critical eye. "Yourself?"

"Thought about it. Never tried, though."

"I can take you out one day if you have a hankering."

"I'd like that. See what my horse can do. He hasn't been on a lot of trails."

"This won't be any run-of-the-mill trail ride." There was a slight challenge in Gary's voice.

Aaron smiled. He liked challenges. "Looking forward to it."

"Leather punch is hanging on the far wall," Gary said and strode off to saddle his horse. With four perfectly matched stockings and a gleaming Sorel coat, the gelding wasn't run-of-the-mill either.

Their plan was to ride every one of the ranch's eight horse

trails winding through the surrounding mountains. They would make sure the trails were, first, accessible and, second, safe. Winter storms were notoriously destructive. Depending on what they found, maintenance crews would be dispatched to clear the trails of debris or repair places where the earth had eroded. Later in the week, Gary and Aaron would lead the riding stock over the same trails, reintroducing the horses before they carried people.

During breakfast that morning, Aaron learned more about Bear Creek Ranch and the many intricacies of its operation than he ever had from his late wife. In many ways, the ranch was like a small, highly organized village. Each resident had a job, from Jake Tucker to Randy and Skunk, and the ranch thrived only when everyone did their job. Aaron had observed a strong camaraderie among the staff, no doubt fueled by the closeness in which they lived, worked and recreated.

Becoming a member of their tight-knit clan, if that was even what he wanted, would require some doing. He might be one of the village leaders, but he hadn't been born into the position, and acceptance didn't come automatically for him.

One aspect of the ranch that had taken him by complete surprise was Jake's living arrangements. Gary apparently assumed Aaron had prior knowledge of Jake's divorce and his move to a house several miles away. Aaron hadn't asked any questions at Gary's casual reference despite a burning curiosity. Faults aside, Aaron's former brother-in-law was a family man through and through. Leaving his daughters must have been a terrible blow and maybe accounted for the anger constantly simmering beneath the surface.

Stepping into the tack room, Aaron looked around. Like everything else in the barn and stables, on the entire ranch for that matter, the place was neat and tidy.

Saddles on racks occupied one entire wall, bridles and halters, another. In the center of the room were back-to-back shelving units. One side held an array of boots in varying sizes and styles, Aaron presumed for guests who didn't bring their own. Cowboy hats and baseball caps were on the other. At the end of one shelf were three child-size riding helmets.

He went over and picked up one of the helmets. Turning it over, he inspected the condition of the straps, buckles and padding. While not new, the helmet was in decent shape and should adequately protect the small head inside it. There were no adult-size helmets in and amongst all the cowboy hats and baseball caps. Did guests not want them or did the ranch not provide them? Aaron intended to find out.

Many of the men he rodeoed with argued helmets didn't make a difference and laughed in the face of anyone suggesting they wear one. They claimed all the safety equipment in the world hadn't helped the actor Christopher Reeves when he suffered his tragic fall from a horse. Aaron wasn't one of those men. If Hailey had been wearing a helmet, she might have survived and he wouldn't be a widower.

It was Aaron's goal, his plan, to see that others *did* survive. Children most especially. For that reason, and to honor Hailey's memory, he'd returned to Bear Creek Ranch.

"Did you find the leather punch?" Gary asked from the doorway.

"Not yet." Aaron replaced the helmet. On impulse, he asked, "Do you have any of these for adults?"

"Helmets? No."

"Can I ask why?"

Gary scratched his chin. "No reason I can think of."

"Have any guests ever requested them?"

"One or two." Gary's expression changed, becoming slightly guarded.

Aaron suspected that while Gary had an obligation to answer all his questions, he didn't want to say anything that might reflect ill on the Tuckers.

"I'm going to recommend to Jake that we purchase some adult helmets." Aaron crossed the room to the wall of tools and removed the leather punch. He turned back around and met Gary's gaze head-on. "That won't be a problem, will it?"

"Not at all."

A safe, noncommittal answer. Aaron wasn't annoyed at Gary. On the contrary. He admired the man for his loyalty to his employer.

The morning ride went smoothly. Gary didn't say much the first hour. He must have grown tired of listening to himself think, because he eventually opened up and began chatting. They rode the two shortest trails first. Using a GPS device, Gary marked locations for the maintenance crews to check.

"What about the hiking and ATV trails?" Aaron asked. They guided their horses around a fallen log.

"Those are to the east and south of the ranch. Horse trails are to the west. We have crews inspecting those as well."

"Are all the trails on ranch property?"

"The shorter ones are. The longer ones cross over onto federal land. We stay in constant contact with the neighboring ranches. They let us know in what areas their cattle are grazing so we can avoid any accidental run-ins."

Gary was in the middle of telling Aaron about the all-day trail rides, which were combined with mini fishing trips, when the radio clipped to his belt emitted a loud beep.

Pulling his horse to a stop, he held the radio to his mouth and said, "Yeah, what's up?"

"Where are you?" a male voice Aaron didn't recognize asked.

"Five miles out. At the base of Windy Pass."

"Hoof it on back. Jake's orders."

"Something wrong?" Gary shifted in his saddle, his steel-gray brows drawn together in a deep V.

"He needs Aaron back here on the double."

"What for?" Aaron asked, feeling himself tense. Jake was up to something.

"Did he say what for?" Gary repeated Aaron's question into the radio.

"Nope. And I didn't ask."

"All right." Gary signed off after giving the caller their ETA.

It was faster to ride the trail to the end than turn around. Once again, he and Aaron talked very little. Probably because the scowl on Aaron's face discouraged conversation. He considered refusing to return then thought better of it. Gary could wind up taking the heat for something that wasn't his fault.

It was past one o'clock when they arrived back at the ranch, and Aaron was hungry. Had Jake's call not come in, he and Gary would have broken for lunch. While Aaron was unsaddling Dollar, Natalie arrived in her golf cart. She parked far enough away not to spook the horses.

Walking toward him, she waved hello.

Because he liked what he saw, he stopped to watch. Her strides were long and her shoulders straight. She might only be a shade above five-six, but she carried herself like someone much taller. Aaron supposed there were guys put off by a woman exuding so much self-confidence. Not him. She had the makings of a true competitor, and Aaron found that a whole lot sexier than tight jeans and a low-cut blouse.

"I'm your ride," she said, going up to Dollar and scratching him between the ears.

"What's going on?"

"I don't know. I was just told to come get you."

"And take me where?"

She followed him when he carried his saddle and bridle into the tack room. "Founders Cabin. It's where Walter and Ida Tucker lived. They were the original owners of the ranch and started the resort."

"Hailey and Jake's grandparents?"

"That's right. After they passed on, their cabin was converted into a sort of museum and conference center."

"Conference center?" Aaron had grabbed a brush on his way out of the tack room. "As in meetings?"

"Yes."

She knew more than she was telling, Aaron would bet on it. But like the rest of her family, her loyalties lay rock solid with the Tuckers.

"We'd best hurry." She checked her watch. "My orders were to take you to the cabin as soon as you and Dad got back."

She was the second person to mention "orders" that day, and Aaron's hackles rose. Jake Tucker really did like to throw his weight around.

"We'll head out as soon as I put up Dollar and grab something to eat." The sandwiches he and Gary packed that morning were still in their saddlebags.

"But Jake said I sh—"

"I don't really care what he said."

Natalie retreated a step, her internal struggle evident on her face.

Aaron swore under his breath. Like her father, she didn't deserve to be put in the middle of his test of wills with Jake, and he was wrong to involve her. But something inside Aaron wanted Natalie to stand up to her boss. Defy him. Choose Aaron over him.

She wouldn't, of course. Not in a million years.

"I'm sorry. I had no right taking my frustration with Jake out on you."

She nodded mutely.

"He has a talent for rubbing me the wrong way."

"I'd say it's mutual." Her expression was mildly reproachful.

Inhaling slowly, Aaron continued in a calmer tone. "Jake's waited this long for me, five more minutes won't make a difference. I'll tell him that you did your best to hurry me along, but I refused. Everyone here will vouch for you." He gestured at the half-dozen hands milling about the stable area, staring at them and trying their darnedest not to be conspicuous about it.

Her father was the exception. He kept a close, unguarded eye on his daughter.

"Okay." Natalie went back to the golf cart, strides still long, shoulders still straight.

He'd won her over. Sort of. Aaron felt a small rush of satisfaction he wasn't entitled to but enjoyed nonetheless.

After returning Dollar to his stall, he grabbed a sandwich and a cold soda, then slid onto the seat beside Natalie.

"Ready?" she asked.

"Let's not keep the man waiting." Which, of course, was exactly what Aaron had done.

She smiled at his joke, and he was glad—very glad, really—there was no residual tension between them.

Aaron wolfed down his sandwich and drink while they drove, which was a good thing. The trip to Founders Cabin was a short one. Located away from the other bunkhouses and main lodge, the cabin sat atop a small hill amid a dense thicket of trees. Not close to anything except a narrow tributary of Bear Creek.

There were two cars and one pickup truck parked outside the cabin. Natalie eased the golf cart between the vehicles and stopped beside a stone walkway leading to the front porch.

Aaron glanced over at her. The guilty expression she wore gave her away.

"Please. I don't want to walk in there blind." He impulsively laid a hand over the one she rested on her leg, and curled his fingers around hers. "Tell me what's going on."

She swallowed, and her gaze traveled to their joined hands, reminding him that he'd once again placed her in an unfair position.

He was about to retract his question when she suddenly blurted, "Jake's called a family meeting. I don't know why or what it's about. He doesn't tell me these things, and he doesn't have to."

"Thanks." Aaron gave her hand a brief squeeze.

He didn't turn around after climbing out of the golf cart, not even when Natalie started the engine and drove away. At the bottom of the porch steps, he paused to read an engraved brass monument sign. It told a short history of Walter and Ida Tucker and how they started the resort. They were an interesting and colorful couple. Aaron was sorry he never had the opportunity to meet them.

But as luck would have it, he was about to meet, and go head-to-head with, their offspring.

Chapter Four

Aaron silently fumed.

His former brother-in-law had been in an all-fired rush to start the meeting only until he arrived. From the moment he stepped over the threshold, Jake had kept everyone waiting while he made one phone call after the other.

To kill time, and avoid the rest of the family seated at the conference table, Aaron wandered the room. He paused in front of a tall bookcase crammed with leather-bound photo albums and removed one at random. Black-and-white snapshots filled every page. Beneath each snapshot someone had written dates, names, and brief descriptions in neat, square lettering. Aaron got his first look at Walter and Ida Tucker, the couple who started the ranch. They were sitting around the outdoor fireplace in front of the dining hall, surrounded by guests.

"My mother and father," a voice from behind him said.

Aaron turned to find a handsome woman with lively eyes and an engaging smile peering over his shoulder. She was the only Tucker in the room to get within ten feet of him, much less talk to him.

"You're Jake's mother?" he asked, looking for a resemblance and finding only a hint of one.

"Heavens, no." The woman's laughter was rich and robust. "If that boy were my son, he'd have a sense of humor and good manners. Being as he's my brother's son, he lacks both." She held out her hand. "I'm Millie Sweetwater."

Aaron thought he just might learn to like Jake's aunt. "I'm Aaron Reyes." He balanced the photo album in the crook of his left arm so that he could shake her hand.

"I know who you are." Her grip was firm, rivaling any man's. Any *young* man's. "Heard you finally decided to grace us with your presence about an hour after you drove onto the property. Got here right under the wire. Another few days and you'd've missed out on all this fun."

"Being a member of the Tucker Family Trust is fun?"

She winked. "From where I sit, it's a hoot."

No doubt about it. He definitely liked Millie.

Liked her even more when he caught Jake glowering at them from the head of a large oak conference table, his cell phone glued to his ear. To his left sat two women who conversed in whispers, probably about him. Jake's cousins, Aaron presumed, which would make them Millie's daughters. On the other side of Jake sat his personal assistant, Alice. She didn't converse with anyone.

"There's Hailey." Millie tapped a finger on one of the snapshots. "That girl always did love horses. It must have been very hard on you when she died."

There was a sadness in Millie's voice that affected Aaron more than her words. It was quickly overshadowed by an anger he'd had no outlet for until now.

"Why the sudden sympathy? You Tuckers barely acknowledged me when Hailey had her accident, much less offered your support."

Millie didn't so much as blink. If anything, she appeared more sorrowful. "Our behavior was appalling. Inexcusable. I, for one, am sorry. But your behavior wasn't all that commendable either," she gently reprimanded. "You should have come to the memorial service."

"Your family didn't want me here."

"We'd have tolerated you."

As they were now? "Is that why you're being nice to me today? To clear your conscience?" Guilt gave Aaron's voice an edge. He should have stood up to Jake and come to Hailey's memorial service instead of hiding behind a wall of grief.

"I deserved that, which is why I won't let your anger ruin our friendship." The twinkle in Millie's eyes reappeared.

Aaron found it hard to stay mad. "You think we're going to be friends?"

"Good ones." She glanced at Jake before patting Aaron's arm. "Would you like to see more pictures of Hailey growing up? There are lots of them. We have albums for every year the resort's been in operation. Ma insisted on it."

"Sure." He grinned. Whatever reason Millie had for being nice to him—and she had one, she was too wily not to—Aaron didn't care as long as it irritated Jake.

She flipped to a new page in the album and said, "There's all the cousins." The six Tucker grandchildren sat grouped together on the floor in front of a huge, elaborately decorated Christmas tree. "Jake's not only the oldest grandchild, he's the only boy." Millie chuckled. "And then the poor man goes and has three daughters. It's not entirely his fault he turned out to be such a stick-in-the-mud. Natalie's no relation but they've known each other their whole lives, and he's as overprotective with her as the rest of the women in his life."

Aaron changed the subject. For some reason he wasn't inclined to talk about Natalie with any of the Tuckers, even the one being nice to him.

"You have four daughters?" He studied Hailey's young face. She'd had the same exuberance about her as a child as she'd had as an adult.

"Oh, yes. Carolina and Rachel over there are my two middle ones. Don't be put off. They're not nearly as mean as they appear," Millie teased. "My oldest is married and lives in Colorado."

"You must miss her." Aaron's own mother complained frequently of his long absences.

"Yes, but the benefit of the family trust is that she's required to spend eight weeks a year here. She splits her weeks up, taking them two at a time. This last time she brought my brand-new granddaughter with her."

"Another girl?" He turned pages as Millie talked.

"It's a family curse."

Aaron's mind went to Hailey. What might the sex of their children have been had she lived?

"My youngest is in the service." Millie glowed with pride. "She's a warrant officer for the army. I have a shop in Payson with Natalie's mother, and I'm also the wedding coordinator for the ranch."

"Is your brother still at the college?"

Because he and Hailey had eloped, Aaron didn't meet his father-in-law until later, though she'd talked a lot about him. When Jake took over the ranch eight years ago, their father followed his lifelong dream of teaching and became an instructor at nearby Gila Community College.

"Are you kidding?" Millie said. "He loves it. Swore running a resort wasn't his thing. Well, guess what he teaches?"

"Business?"

She harrumphed. "Hospitality and tourism management."

Aaron wasn't sorry his former father-in-law had to miss the meeting. Not that he'd expected the red-carpet treatment from him, either. Only after he and Hailey were married did he understand his wife's reluctance to invite her family to the ceremony. The Tuckers weren't thrilled with her chosen groom, especially her father and brother, and let her know it.

Aaron closed the photo album and returned it to its slot. He was enjoying talking to Millie but growing impatient with Jake's stall tactics. "Why exactly are we here?"

"A family meeting. Jake's authority to act on behalf of the trust has limitations. Whatever he has on the agenda must require a majority vote. If not, we wouldn't have been summoned. Didn't our attorney explain everything to you?"

"I wasn't paying much attention." Aaron had existed in a fog for months after Hailey's death.

"Well, if you have any questions, call him. I can give you his number."

"Jake doesn't need me for a majority vote. He's gotten along so far without me."

"Ah, but he does. The trust stipulates that any members residing on the ranch are required to attend meetings. If he weren't bound by the trust, you'd still be riding the trails with Gary."

"Is everyone ready?" Jake snapped shut his cell phone and dropped it into his shirt pocket.

"Waiting on you," Millie chirped.

She and Aaron wandered to the table and chose seats. Aaron selected his because it was next to Millie and directly across from Jake. They immediately locked gazes.

Aaron wasn't the type to fold under pressure. It was a quality he'd honed, one that had enabled him to rise from a nobody at age nineteen to a national champion at age twenty-four.

Jake broke eye contact in order to distribute papers to everyone present. He explained to the group how the company they leased their fleet of ATVs from had waited until the last minute to announce a rate hike, one that far exceeded the ranch's budget.

Options were discussed, everything from locating another leasing company to paying the higher rate. Aaron listened far more than he contributed. There wasn't much he could add. And though he hated to admit it, Jake clearly was no dummy when it came to running the ranch. After a final round of discussion, a vote was taken.

The meeting was at an end when Aaron finally spoke up. "I have something I want to talk about."

"You do?" One corner of Jake's mouth curved up, either in amusement or disdain. It was hard to tell. His smile didn't differ much from his frown. "Does it involve spending money?"

"Could."

Jake made a show of checking his watch. "Can it wait until

our regular monthly meeting on the twentieth? Alice will put it on the agenda."

"This won't take long." Aaron's insistence increased in proportion to Jake's attempts to blow him off.

"I have a three o'clock appointment in town," Jake said with a finality that implied his patience was at an end.

"Play nice, Jake," Millie warned, all trace of her earlier congeniality gone. "Aaron has the right to initiate a discussion. Same as any of us."

Aaron understood then what she'd meant about shaking things up.

If Jake was annoyed with his aunt, he covered it well. "Since when have the conditions of the trust interested you?"

"Since yesterday." She broke into the wide, sassy smile of a person truly enjoying herself. "You're an excellent manager of the family business, Jake. Better even than your father. But let's be honest. You can also be a pain in the rear."

One cousin looked away, the other one giggled.

Jake's scowl lasted a mere two seconds. "If I am a pain in the rear, I inherited it from you."

"One of my finer traits." Millie laughed.

Aaron had to hand it to them. The Tuckers may not be an easy family to belong to, but their bond was strong.

Not unlike his own family.

He made a silent vow to visit home more often. The majority of his siblings and their families still lived in and around the Phoenix area and those who didn't would make the drive—hopefully. In escaping his grief over Hailey, he's pushed away the people who loved him the most. Maybe it wasn't too late to change…

"Fine, Reyes. What is it you want to talk to us about?"

Jake's abrupt question roused Aaron. "Riding helmets."

"Really," Jake said with practiced neutrality.

"I found three children's helmets in the tack room this morning. There were no adult helmets."

"Don't recall we've ever had a need for them."

"I asked Gary Forrester, and he told me a couple guests have requested them."

"What exactly are you proposing?" Jake sat back in his chair, but there was nothing relaxed about him. Beneath the table, one knee bounced, and he held his pen in a death grip.

"That we buy three more children's helmets and six adult helmets. I also think we should posts signs in the main lodge and at the stables, informing guests that helmets are available should they want one."

"We?"

Aaron paused. Was the slip unconscious or had he finally begun to accept his position in the family?

"How much do helmets cost?" Carolina asked.

"For good ones, a hundred to a hundred and fifty each."

"The yearly budget's already been approved," Jake said firmly. "We don't have any extra funds."

"It's a thousand dollars, Jake," Millie answered with equal firmness. "I think we can find a place in the budget for that without throwing the entire ranch finances into turmoil. Alice, do you have the new budget on your laptop?"

"Yes, ma'am." She grabbed the wireless mouse and began clicking.

"You might save that much in liability insurance," Aaron suggested. "Talk to your agent."

Jake leaned forward and propped his elbows on the table. "Are you an insurance expert now?"

"No, but I've carried plenty of it over the years."

"On Hailey?"

"On me," Aaron answered steadily and fought to remain calm.

Jake was baiting him, Aaron recognized the ploy. He'd had it used on him by his four brothers and two sisters—and used it on them in return—all the years they were growing up.

"Hey," Carolina interjected. "No reason to go all testosterone on us."

"It's not a bad idea," Rachel appealed to Jake. "Seriously."

"Guests may get the idea riding isn't safe."

"Sometimes riding isn't safe. We all know that." Carolina glanced at Aaron.

He wondered if he'd gained another ally or at least some ground.

"Guests may also feel reassured by the availability of helmets," she said with noticeably growing confidence. "That their safety is our top concern."

Jake's jaw visibly clenched. "This isn't anything we should jump into without careful consideration."

"I agree." Millie smiled approvingly. "I make a motion that we table the discussion of purchasing helmets until the next regular meeting. In the meantime, Alice can contact our insurance agent, see if we qualify for a rate break. And Aaron can obtain prices so we know exactly what the cost will be."

She was no dummy when it came to running the ranch either.

Aaron figured now was a good time to drop his final bombshell. "What if the helmets were free of charge?"

That got everyone's attention.

"You have some?" Carolina asked.

"No. But I know where we might be able to get them."

"Where?"

Jake snorted.

Carolina bristled. "Honestly, Jake. If we can get the helmets at no cost, what's the harm in providing them?"

"Nothing's for free. There's always a catch."

"No catch," Aaron said. "I know of an organization that promotes equestrian safety. We can apply to them for a grant and if they approve our request, the helmets are ours. No charge."

"What organization is that?" Jake's gaze narrowed with suspicion.

Aaron met it head-on. "The Hailey Reyes Foundation for Equestrian Safety. I'm the chairman."

Four faces stared at him with expressions ranging from surprise to shock.

The fifth, Millie's, radiated pure delight.

NATALIE PACED the lobby floor, beside herself with frustration. Her usually complacent, good-natured baby had been crying nonstop for the last hour and showed no signs of wearing herself out. Natalie, on the other hand, was exhausted.

For the second time since she'd returned from the family meeting ten minutes ago, Alice opened her office door, stuck her head out and said, "Can't you do something about her crying?" then shut the door with unnecessary force.

"Don't you think I would if I could?" Natalie muttered under her breath.

She tried not to think harshly of Alice. Having a baby in the office was distracting to anyone, and it didn't exactly give the professional impression Alice prided herself on. In Natalie's opinion, Jake's personal assistant took herself and her job too seriously. But in all fairness, she'd come into a situation where she was the newcomer and everyone else had been with the ranch for years and years. That could be intimidating and give a person reason to think they needed to prove themselves.

All the more reason for Natalie to be more understanding of her coworker and find reliable day care. She circled the couch in front of the reception area, Shiloh resting on her shoulder, her cries escalating to an eardrum-piercing level. Thank goodness Jake had left for his appointment in town.

Natalie's frustration escalated. She didn't know what else to check. Shiloh's diaper wasn't wet. She wasn't hungry, or at least, she refused to nurse. She had no temperature, no runny nose, no spit-up and no other outward signs of being sick. Three months was too young to start teething, wasn't it?

Jake's daughter, Briana, was due to arrive in fifteen minutes. Natalie couldn't possibly hand over Shiloh to her babysitter until she'd quieted down.

In desperation, Natalie pulled out her cell phone and called her mother at the store.

"Good afternoon, Trinkets and Treasure."

"Mom! Help."

"Natalie, honey, what's wrong?"

"Shiloh won't stop crying."

Deana laughed.

"This isn't funny."

"You don't know how lucky you are. Shiloh isn't normal."

"Thanks," Natalie said sarcastically.

"That's not what I mean and you know it. She's usually so easy. You haven't had to endure the difficulties most mothers do."

"Well, it's looking like my abnormal baby is now normal." Natalie continued circling the couch. "Got any suggestions?"

"Your grandmother used to feed us kids a teaspoon of whiskey."

"I'm not giving Shiloh alcohol!" Natalie said, appalled.

"If Mom didn't have whiskey, she'd use chamomile tea."

"You're no help."

"I'm teasing." Deana laughed again. "Have you tried putting her in her car seat and driving her around the ranch?"

"I can't leave. I'm on duty."

"Rocking her?"

"Yes." Twice Natalie had sat with Shiloh in the wicker rocker on the front porch.

"Putting her down and letting her cry herself to sleep?"

"Alice complained."

"Walking her in her stroller? Oh, wait, you're on duty."

"And besides, my stroller isn't here."

Natalie was verging on frantic. Jake was due back at four-thirty. He might stop being so generous with her if he had to listen to a squalling baby. She reminded herself to breathe deeply. Shiloh probably sensed her frustration and was responding to it.

"What about moving her portable crib to a different location? Maybe a change of scenery will help."

"Hmm. That's a good idea. Thanks, Mom."

Natalie returned to the storage room after hanging up with her mother. Repositioning Shiloh in her left arm, she grabbed the edge of the lightweight crib and dragged it through the door to the front porch. The scraping sound quieted Shiloh, but only for a minute. As soon as Natalie had the crib in position, Shiloh started up again.

Checking her diaper one last time, Natalie laid the baby down in the crib and pulled the wicker rocker over to sit in. She then wound up a musical teddy bear and put it in the crib next to Shiloh, talking soothingly all the while.

Five minutes later, Shiloh was still crying, and Natalie had begun to worry that something was seriously wrong. The baby's face was beet red and her cries had become thready and hoarse.

Maybe she should call her pediatrician. Jumping up, she dashed inside to fetch the number from her Rolodex. She wasn't gone three minutes. But by the time she returned, two things had happened: Shiloh wasn't alone on the porch, and she'd stopped crying.

Aaron was with her.

He sat in the rocking chair, his large hand inside the crib, tenderly stroking Shiloh's tiny forehead and singing to her in Spanish. Shiloh didn't seem to care that his voice was gravelly and a bit off-key. She stared at him, transfixed—and utterly silent.

She wasn't the only one.

Natalie froze, watching, not sure what to make of the situation. At first, her maternal instincts kicked in, and she had to squash the impulse to rush over and snatch her baby away from this almost stranger's clutches. The singing stopped her. Then touched her.

Shiloh interacted so seldom with men. None, really, other than Natalie's father. As much as Shiloh's grandfather adored her, he wasn't very comfortable around little babies and broke into a cold sweat every time he so much as held her.

Not so, Aaron. He soothed Shiloh's crying jag as if he'd been around babies his entire life. Maybe he had. Despite being the object of much gossip, no one knew a whole lot about him, including the Tuckers.

Natalie was almost reluctant to approach Aaron. Shiloh

might start crying again if he stopped singing. She stood directly behind him, thinking he hadn't noticed her. But then he spoke, his voice almost as soft as his singing.

"She's asleep."

"Really?" Natalie whispered and stepped closer, afraid to hope. "She's been crying for over an hour. I was getting ready to call the doctor."

Peering around Aaron, she saw that her daughter was indeed asleep, and her shoulders sagged with relief. Alice would be thrilled. And Natalie could finally get some work done. She glanced down the road and spotted Briana approaching in the distance. Perfect timing.

"Thank you," Natalie said.

Aaron stood and slowly backed up, not taking his eyes off Shiloh. "I hope you don't mind. I know mothers don't like just anyone coming around their babies."

"It's all right." And it was all right. Natalie couldn't explain the sense of security she felt with Aaron. The same instinct that compelled her to protect her baby also told her this man intended no harm.

"My mother used to sing that song to us," he said.

"It's beautiful." His inability to carry a decent tune hadn't spoiled the lullaby's loveliness or impressive calming effects.

"I'm from a large family. Seven kids. My mom had a lot of practice getting babies to sleep."

He spun around rather suddenly, and the next thing Natalie knew, they were standing face-to-face. Her heart gave a small leap at his proximity.

"I…um…sing to her…too. Doesn't work quite so well."

"She was having a bad day. We all do every now and then."

Was he referring to himself? The meeting with the Tuckers couldn't have gone well, if Alice's cranky mood was any indication.

Natalie knew she should move. Briana had reached the base of the small hill leading to the main lodge and would be climbing the porch steps soon. Natalie's feet, however, remained glued to the floor. So, apparently, did Aaron's. She swore she felt his touch, warm and lingering and so intense the hairs on her arm stood on end. Yet he did no more than gaze at her.

"Is there something I can help you with inside?" she asked weakly. He had to have come to the main lodge for a reason.

"I'm meeting with Alice to go over some prices."

"Okay." She didn't ask for what. His business with Alice wasn't her concern. "I'll be at my desk if you need anything."

"A cot, maybe."

Natalie smiled. "Changed your mind, huh?"

"That couch isn't exactly good for my beauty sleep, and I need all the help I can get."

He was joking, of course. How could he not be? The man was incredibly good-looking. Especially now that she saw him up close. So very close.

"I'll take care of it right away," she murmured and unstuck her feet just as Briana approached the stone walkway. Had Natalie delayed one second longer, Briana would have had quite a tale to tell her father.

Walking over to the steps to meet her babysitter, Natalie watched Aaron go inside from the corner of her eye and a moment later heard the door shut. Only then did her heart cease beating erratically.

Jake Tucker might detest Aaron, but his little sister hadn't and neither did Natalie. With each encounter she had with him, it became clearer and clearer how Hailey could have given her love to him so quickly and so easily.

If Natalie wasn't careful, she, like her boss's sister, like her own little daughter, would fall under the spell of Aaron Reyes.

Chapter Five

"I personally checked it out," Alice Gilbert said with a self-appointed authority that didn't match her petite size. "The Hailey Reyes Foundation is legitimate."

She led a group of eight managers, which included Natalie, down the stone walkway and away from the main lodge. Every area of the ranch was represented in the group. Guest services, food services, guest amenities, maintenance, landscape and administration. They were meeting up with Jake and the other members of the Tucker family to finalize the details of the opening-day celebration and to walk the grounds.

Natalie could hardly believe the new season was upon them. The weeks had flown by. Especially this last one since Aaron arrived. She wondered if he'd be at the meeting. No, she *hoped* he'd be at the meeting. He'd been scarce lately, spending most of his time at the stables with her father. She didn't dare inquire about Aaron. Her father was no dummy. He'd guess right away her interest went beyond casual, which it did.

"I, for one, think it's very sweet what he did for Hailey," Olivia murmured out of the side of her mouth.

"Yes," Natalie agreed.

She didn't mention Alice's earlier remark that the foundation was probably a tax shelter Aaron created to write off expenses. Anyone looking at Aaron would know the man had no expenses to write off. He drove a ten-year-old truck, pulled a twelve-year-old trailer and lived out of a duffel bag. Even his laptop was old.

When the group reached the outdoor fireplace, everyone took a seat on the long, circular concrete bench. While Alice distributed the schedules they would be going over, family members showed up one by one, in cars or trucks mostly. One person arrived on horseback. Aaron. Natalie stole a moment away from reading the schedule to admire the sight of him in the saddle. A small, involuntary sigh escaped her lips.

No doubt about it. She had a weakness for good-looking cowboys—which is what got her in trouble with Shiloh's father. Wait. Not trouble, she quickly reminded herself. Having a child was the best thing to ever happen to her, and she wouldn't change her life for the world.

This good-looking cowboy, however, was different from Shiloh's father. Altogether different. He was Jake's late sister's husband.

A meeting around the fireplace to discuss the opening day celebration was a yearly tradition on the ranch. Jake always kicked off the meeting with a speech designed to get them excited about the new season.

Natalie half listened. Most of her efforts were applied to watching Aaron, who, having tied his horse to a nearby hitching rail, stood behind the bench and off to the side.

Apparently, she'd far from mastered the technique of discreet observation, for Olivia leaned over and whispered, "He's very handsome."

Natalie played dumb. "Who?"

"Him." Olivia nodded at Aaron. "The one you keep staring at."

"I'm not staring."

Olivia rolled her eyes.

Natalie continued pretending to listen to Jake's speech. She lasted a full minute before her attention drifted once more to Aaron. This time, he caught her looking at him. Neither of them turned away. Seconds ticked by. An elbow in her side broke Natalie's concentration.

"Pay attention, *chiquita.*"

Natalie was paying rapt attention, but to the wrong man.

Jake ended his speech a few minutes later, after which Alice took charge again. She explained that the opening day celebration would have a few small changes from previous years and detailed each manager's duties. Afternoon games of horseshoes, badminton, a fishing tournament and a scavenger hunt would still be followed by a dinner. Instead of the usual barbecue chicken, they were going to have a chili cook-off. The Payson radio station had agreed to a live broadcast and were sending a celebrity DJ to judge.

Alice might not be a favorite among her coworkers but no one could deny she'd done an admirable job generating publicity for the ranch. While she reviewed the rest of the day's events, the occasional employee meandered past, heading to the dining hall. Another tradition held this day was the annual company meeting. It was the only time during the busy season all the employees on the ranch gathered together in one place and at one time.

Finally, Alice dismissed the group. Everyone stood, stretched and began to meander toward the dining hall to join the employees. Natalie tried to listen as Olivia rambled on about the chili cook-off and the additional work required of her and her staff. Natalie's interest, however, wandered elsewhere.

It stopped wandering the moment Aaron fell into step beside her.

Nodding at her and Olivia, he said, "Thanks for the bed."

"You're welcome." Rather than a cot, Natalie had located him a roll-away bed. "Is Teresa cutting you any slack?"

"I'm winning her over slowly but surely."

Teresa would have to be made of stone not to fall prey to Aaron's easy charm. Something, Natalie reminded herself, *she* should be careful of.

Olivia slowed her steps and slipped away, leaving Natalie and Aaron walking alone. She swallowed, acutely aware of him. His height. His breadth. The corded muscles of his forearms, revealed by the rolled-back sleeves of his work shirt.

The fine dusting of dark hair on those bare arms. Since Natalie wasn't made of stone either, she responded to his undeniable masculinity with a purely feminine tingling in her middle.

"How's Shiloh doing?" he asked.

"No more crying, thank goodness. Not like the other day."

"Good." He flashed a grin that managed to be more sexy than humorous. Or was it merely the effect he had on her? "If you need my help again, just holler."

His hand brushed her arm. Accidentally or intentionally, Natalie wasn't sure.

"Thanks," she muttered, assuring herself the veiled invitation in his voice was a figment of her overactive imagination.

"So, can anyone enter these opening-day events or just guests and visitors?"

"Anyone." Natalie breathed easier, glad for the change of topic. "Are you thinking of entering?"

"The chili cook-off. My mother's an incredible cook."

"And she taught you everything she knows?"

"Almost everything." His grin softened, became more intimate. "The rest I learned on my own."

The tingling in Natalie's middle returned.

"My mother's the smartest woman I know. And the hardest worker. My dad left after my youngest brother was born. She raised us kids single-handed, got every one of us through high school whether we wanted to graduate or not."

Natalie chided herself for assuming the warm look in his eyes was for her. Aaron had been recalling his mother and the sacrifices she'd made for her children.

"She sounds like a wonderful person."

"You remind me of her."

"I do?"

"Yes."

Okay. She wasn't assuming. The warmth in those incredibly dark eyes of his really was directed at her.

Natalie didn't realize she'd come to a standstill until he put a hand on her elbow and gently guided her onto the first step of the walkway leading to the dining hall. His fingers were gentle, yet firm, and without the slightest trace of force.

Her father owned a collection of rodeo DVDs, some of them featuring Aaron. She'd studied the segments of him riding closely, watched him stay seated on horses that were four-legged tornadoes hell-bent on throwing him off. The only thing between him and certain injury was the hand that gripped the rope. The same hand that had tenderly stroked her crying daughter's forehead and now held her arm.

What else was that hand capable of?

Natalie instinctively understood that Aaron could evoke a sensual response in her like she'd never felt before with a simple stroke of his fingers. He was doing as much to her right this moment and he only held her elbow.

With great effort, she placed one foot in front of the other and continued walking. People were bound to notice if she didn't get a move on.

"You really should enter the chili cook-off," she said. "It'll be fun."

"Are there prizes?"

"Plaques. Nice ones. My mom and I make them. Well, Mom designs them. I help."

"All the more incentive for me to enter."

"Jake is reigning horseshoes champion. He's won the last four years."

"You don't say."

Natalie swore she detected a hint of challenge in Aaron's voice. "Do you play?"

"I have. Once or twice. I'm a better cook than horseshoe player."

"And a better bronc rider than cook?"

"Guess we'll find out during the cook-off."

They reached the door to the dining hall. Aaron held it open and waited for Natalie to enter. They were one of the last to join the meeting. Most heads turned in their direction and a noticeable hum went through the room.

Natalie straightened. She'd done nothing inappropriate, nothing to feel ashamed of. Yet, for some reason, all the attention she and Aaron attracted caused a giant knot in her stomach.

When she veered right toward where her father was sitting, Aaron followed—because he worked with her father, she told herself, not because he wanted to sit with her. Damn. She should go find Olivia. Wait, no. If Aaron followed her, she'd have no excuse to give people for why he had. Better this way.

She made an attempt at casual conversation for the benefit of anyone within earshot. "I heard about the foundation you started in Hailey's memory. That's a nice thing to do. She'd be very pleased."

"Did you know her well?" Aaron asked.

"Not like Carolina and her sisters. Hailey was a little older than the rest of us. She used to babysit my sister and me before she away to college." Natalie's father waved them over. She dropped into the chair beside him, greatly relieved when Aaron sat across from her. "I'm really sorry about the accident. The foundation will do a lot to keep her memory alive."

"I'm hoping for more than that. We have an entire campaign designed to educate youths on the importance of wearing adequate safety equipment when riding." Aaron's glance encompassed everyone in the vicinity and included them in the conversation, for which Natalie was glad. The stir they'd created when they entered the dining hall together appeared to have died down.

"Can't be easy getting kids to wear helmets," Teresa said. She sat beside Skunk, who, as usual, listened to his iPod and talked very little.

"It isn't. There's a prevalent attitude among kids that wearing helmets isn't cool. And that attitude isn't restricted to horseback riding."

Aaron spoke confidently and skillfully, as if he was accustomed to addressing an audience. Being chairman of the foundation, he probably was.

"English riders have always worn helmets," Teresa said. She appeared interested in what Aaron was saying.

"Some endurance and trail riders, too." He nodded at Natalie's father. "But it hasn't caught on with western riders. We're working on changing that."

Alice went to the podium that had been set up at the front of the dining hall for the meeting and announced they would start in a couple of minutes.

"I'm going to grab a cold drink." Aaron rose from his chair. "Would anyone else like something?"

A couple people took him up on his offer, including Natalie. She sat back, feeling better by the second. His talk about the foundation had successfully deflected attention from her. Or so she thought.

Her father bent close to avoid being overheard. "I haven't interfered in your life or told you what to do since you were seventeen years old. Not even when you took up with that fellow last year at the rodeo." He reached up and tugged on a loose lock of her hair. "So forgive your old man this once."

"For what, Dad?"

"Be careful, sweetheart." The worry lines bracketing his mouth deepened. "Don't get involved with Aaron Reyes."

"I'm not," she insisted.

"Not yet. But after seeing the besotted look on both your faces, I'm worried it's only a matter of time."

"You're wrong."

"I hope." He shrugged, though the gesture was anything but casual. "Because you've got a hell of a good thing going here, and I'd hate to see you screw it up."

NATALIE PUSHED THROUGH the front door of the main lodge, a cool breeze at her back, and ran to catch the phone ringing at her workstation.

"Good morning, Bear Creek Ranch. How may I assist you?"

While the caller inquired about vacancies in the month of March, Natalie booted up her computer and checked the log.

"Yes, sir. We have a two-bedroom cabin available that week. It's one of my favorites and has a lovely view of the creek."

She answered several more questions about rates and amenities. Eventually, the caller booked a reservation. Natalie liked starting the day off on a positive note, especially when the previous one hadn't ended all that great.

Once again she found herself the center of ranch gossip and disliking it even more than before. Whatever it took, be it ducking behind trees or pretending to be deaf, dumb and blind, she'd avoid Aaron in the coming weeks. Eventually, the tongue waggers would lose interest, at least until another not-so-lucky someone landed in the hot seat. And besides, all the employees would be too busy preparing for the opening-day celebration to engage in frivolous speculation about her and Aaron. Or, so she hoped.

"Morning."

Natalie looked up from her computer to see Alice marching across the lobby.

She stopped at the edge of the reception counter and asked, "Did the mail come yesterday?"

"You know, I forgot all about it." The annual meeting had run late, and Natalie did no more than close up before heading home to her cabin and Shiloh. "It's over there." She pointed to a tray by the white guest phone.

Alice retrieved the stack and began thumbing through it. "Huh!" She withdrew a large manila envelope. "This is for you." A flicker of interest lit her eyes.

"Really?" Natalie walked over to the counter and took the envelope from Alice's hands. Strange. It was from an attorney in Wichita. Well, attorneys did book vacations. But why did the envelope have her name on it? She must have talked to the sender about a reservation and since forgot.

Returning to her chair, she tore open the envelope and tried to quell the nervous quivering in her stomach. It only got worse as she read the first few lines of the enclosed cover letter.

Dear Ms. Forrester, I'm writing to you on behalf of my client, Drew Nolan.

Shiloh's father! Natalie's fingers began to tremble and her heart raced. Drew had hired an attorney. He was *not* getting custody of Shiloh and taking her to Wichita. Natalie would fight him tooth and nail. Hire the best professional help she could find.

She continued reading, only vaguely aware she wasn't alone. Sentence fragments leaped off the page at her.

Mr. Nolan's forthcoming marriage…
…his wish to abdicate his rights in regards to your daughter, Shiloh.
To this end, he will pay all related legal expenses up to…
…sign and return the enclosed documents.

Drew didn't want custody of Shiloh. He didn't want their daughter at all. And he was getting married! Something he'd refused to consider when they were together.

Natalie's head swam, leaving her disoriented. She set the papers down in her lap.

"Are you all right?" Alice asked, concern in her voice.

"Yes." But Natalie didn't feel all right.

She should be thrilled. Relieved if nothing else. She hadn't wanted Drew in her and Shiloh's lives, not after his disappointing reaction to her pregnancy. But instead, she was confused. And troubled. Lately, she'd been wondering if she was too quick sending Drew away and admonishing herself for not leaving the door open. Now, Drew had slammed it shut in her face. No, Shiloh's face.

"You sure?" Alice came around the counter. "Because you look like somebody just died."

"Shiloh's father wants to abdicate his rights." The words tumbled out before Natalie could stop them. She blamed her distressed state of mind.

"Hurray," Alice said snidely. "Good riddance to bad rubbish."

"You're right." Natalie rubbed her forehead. "But—"

"But what? You kicked him to the curb last spring. This simply makes it official."

She couldn't explain without sounding stupid. It was one thing for her not to want Drew around because he hadn't shown himself to be good father material. Another thing for him to completely sever all ties to their daughter.

Natalie had always assumed that one day Shiloh would ask about her father. She might want to contact him, establish a relationship with him. Natalie was prepared to accept that even if she didn't like it. And who knew? Drew might one day change his mind and want to make their daughter a part of his life.

Family medical history was also a consideration. Children sometimes got sick. Biological relatives were needed for transplants or information or…or…

Natalie had trouble focusing.

"Consult a lawyer before you agree to anything," Alice advised. "I'm sure the family trust attorney will help you, though you may want to hire an expert in the field."

"I suppose you're right."

"You don't want to give up something important, like child support."

"He doesn't pay any now."

"Oh." Alice's frown smacked of disapproval.

"I don't need it," Natalie answered hotly, compelled to defend herself.

"Not now. But what if things change? You could fall and break your legs and not be able to work for a year. The Tuckers aren't going to support you forever."

True. Her six-week paid maternity leave had been generous, but she couldn't expect them to take care of her indefinitely if something serious happened.

A small moan escaped her lips. "I need time. To think."

"Absolutely. Don't make any rash decisions. And let me know if you need anything."

Natalie's head shot up at Alice's last remark. She actually sounded sincere and concerned for once. As if she cared.

"I will. Thanks."

Alice may not have been Natalie's first choice for someone

to confide in, but doing so had a calming effect. Enough so Natalie could start planning a course of action. Come lunch break, the phone calls would commence.

Further conversation between Natalie and Alice was postponed by the door to the lobby opening and the appearance of a stranger. He strode purposefully toward the reception counter.

Natalie stood and put on her best greet-the-customer face. "Good morning."

Alice gave him a thorough up and down.

He reached into his jacket pocket and produced a business card. Smiling, he gave the card to Natalie. "Jalen DeLaine. I'm a field inspector with Waterford Insurance."

The name rang no bells with Natalie but obviously did with Alice.

She stepped forward. "I'm Mr. Tucker's assistant. Can I help you with something?"

"Is he available?" the man asked, giving Alice a card as well.

"He hasn't arrived yet this morning."

Jake lived in a small house on some acreage a few miles up the highway. Ellen was supposed to move out when their youngest graduated high school, enabling Jake to return to the ranch and his home. If for any reason she left prior to that, Jake would automatically get full custody of his daughters.

Though many would consider the arrangement strange and wonder why Jake would leave the ranch, Natalie knew it was important to her boss that his children grow up in the same home he had, enjoy the same country lifestyle, remain near the close-knit Tucker family. She'd been blessed with the same privileges herself and intended to pass them on to Shiloh as well.

"Can you reach him for me?" Jalen DeLaine asked, his smile polite yet devoid of warmth.

"I'll try. Is he expecting you?"

"This is an unannounced inspection in response to a call we received."

Alice gave a tiny jerk but recovered quickly. "Excuse me a minute. I'll be right back." She disappeared into her office, shutting the door behind her.

"Can I get you some coffee while you're waiting?" Natalie asked automatically. Her mind was still on the letter from Drew's attorney.

"No, thanks. I had two cups already on the way up here."

She read his business card and noted his office was located in Phoenix.

"Would you care for a seat while you're waiting?"

"I'd prefer to stand, if you don't mind. Two hours behind the wheel is plenty for me."

Alice emerged from her office and approached the reception desk, visibly disconcerted. "I'm sorry. Mr. Tucker is having outpatient surgery this morning in Payson. He won't be in all day. His cousin, Carolina, another one of the owners, asks if you can reschedule."

Outpatient surgery? Jake hadn't mentioned anything of the kind.

Alice, chewing on a thumbnail, appeared every bit as surprised as Natalie.

"If I rescheduled," Jalen Delaine replied smoothly, "it wouldn't be an unannounced inspection." His smile dimmed. "Is there another family member I can meet with?"

"Not anyone who can be here quickly. The senior Mr. Tucker is teaching at Gila College. Millie Sweetwater is at her store in Payson. Her other two daughters don't live on the ranch. I can try to locate Rachel."

"What about Aaron Reyes?"

Natalie's stomach gave a little jump. Alice's reaction was considerably stronger. "I don't know where Mr. Reyes is this morning," she said crisply.

"He does live on the ranch?"

"Um…yes."

"Call him." Jalen DeLaine's tone cooled by a good twenty degrees.

Alice looked at Natalie, her lips pressed tightly together. Her expression said she didn't want Aaron taking Jalen DeLaine around the ranch. Not without Jake present.

Their visitor placed his hands on the reception counter and leaned forward. He was a big man with the ability to intimidate. "Unless you arrange for one of the owners to take me around the ranch in the next fifteen minutes, I'm going to file a report with the carrier."

Alice retreated a step, beaten. She turned to Natalie. "See if you can find Aaron."

Natalie picked up the phone on her desk and called the stables. She got one of the hands, who told her Aaron and her father were behind the barn, overseeing the hay delivery.

"Give him a message," Natalie said. "Tell him to drive up here to the main lodge on the double."

"Something wrong?"

She snuck a discreet glance at Jalen DeLaine. "Yes."

Fifteen minutes later, Aaron's old pickup truck chugged to a stop in front of the lodge. While waiting, Jalen DeLaine had paced the lobby, leafing through ranch flyers and studying the oil paintings adorning the walls.

At the sound of tires on gravel, Alice flew out her office. "I'd be more than happy to accompany you and Mr. Reyes around the ranch."

"Thank you, but that won't be necessary." DeLaine grabbed his briefcase off the old leather couch and nodded at the two women. "Appreciate your help."

The second the door closed, Natalie and Alice dashed to the window and spied through the green-checkered curtains like a pair of schoolgirls. Aaron stepped out of the truck and walked to meet Jalen DeLaine halfway. The two men shook hands and immediately engaged in conversation. A minute later, Aaron showed DeLaine to his truck.

"Jake isn't going to be happy about this," Alice murmured as the men drove off.

Natalie couldn't agree more.

First the letter from Drew's attorney. Then Jake's mysterious surgery. Last, the unannounced inspection from the insurance company.

All in all, it had been one unsettling morning.

Chapter Six

"What do you bet Aaron called the insurance company?" Jake muttered then squeezed his eyes closed when a sharp stab of pain sliced through him.

"What do you bet he didn't?" his cousin Carolina retorted. "If you remember, we did have Alice contact them about a rate break for using helmets."

"So now they want to see what other safety precautions we're not utilizing and stick us with an increase."

"Or which ones we *are* utilizing and reward us with a discount."

"Why are you on his side?"

"I'm on the ranch's side."

Jake pressed a hand to his tender abdomen. His cousin was no dummy. She'd received the call concerning the insurance inspector about the time Jake's doctor was administering anesthesia. She wisely chose to withhold the information until they were halfway home. If Jake had learned about the inspector's visit while still in the surgical center, he might have ripped out his tubes and needles and demanded they leave that instant.

One thing stopped him from urging Carolina to put the pedal to the metal. Every bump they hit, every twist in the road, triggered a wave of pain that would have sent him to his knees if he weren't buckled in.

"Go straight to the ranch," he said through gritted teeth.

Carolina took her eyes off the road long enough to gawk at him. "Are you out of your mind? You just had hernia surgery."

"I'm okay."

"The hell you are. You can't stand up straight. You couldn't even dress yourself without the nurse's help."

"I want to meet with the inspector before he leaves. See what Aaron screwed up."

"How do you know he screwed up?"

"Dammit, Carolina."

"Overdo it, and you'll be right back at the surgical center," she warned. "You heard what the doctor said."

"I like living on the edge. And don't tell anyone about the surgery. Got it?"

She grimaced. "Too late."

"Who knows?"

"Just Alice. And only that you were having an outpatient procedure. Not what kind."

"I wanted to keep this quiet."

"Well, I couldn't help it. The whole inspector thing threw me off." She removed a bottled water from the cup holder beside her and took a sip. "Why do you have to be all secretive anyway? One look at you and everyone's going to know something's wrong."

"My health is my business. Nobody else's." When he'd scheduled the procedure two weeks earlier, he intended to tell a few people besides Carolina about it. That changed when Aaron showed up. Nothing was going to keep Jake away from the ranch for more than a few hours. Not while his former brother-in-law was there.

"Those damn helmets," Jake complained, "are going to—"

"Those damn helmets are merely an excuse. If not for them, you'd find something else to argue with Aaron about."

"I have plenty of choices."

"Fine. He made a few mistakes. But so did you. So did we all."

Despite their nearly eight-year age difference, Jake had

always been closer to Carolina than any of her sisters. She clearly reciprocated the feeling, treating him more like an older brother than a cousin. In a small way, she filled the void left by Hailey's death.

"He should have come to her funeral."

"And you should have made him feel included. Not like an ax murderer responsible for her death."

"Water under the bridge." Jake held his gut and prayed for smoother road ahead—that, or a quick death to put an end to his suffering. Why hadn't those pain pills taken effect yet?

"It goes both ways."

"Okay. I'm a jerk. Enroll me in a 12-step program."

"You can be a jerk."

He grunted.

Carolina's demeanor softened. "But it's because you care. We know that and adore you for it and we wouldn't have you any other way."

"She married him for the wrong reasons."

"Since when is falling in love the wrong reason?"

"Love had very little to do with it. She wanted a husband, and he wanted a free ride."

"You're wrong, Jake."

"Am I?" He shifted in the seat, trying to minimize his discomfort.

"Yes," Carolina said firmly. "I didn't meet Aaron until Hailey died, but I talked to her often before that. She was head over heels in love with him and happy. Really happy."

Jake said nothing.

"And as far as the free ride goes, we both know the trust hasn't been providing its members with enough income to live on for the past few years."

The quarterly payments would be a little bigger, thought Jake glumly, if Aaron had done the decent thing—the *right* thing—and forfeited his share back to the family.

"I don't like him hanging around Natalie."

"News flash, Jake. She's hanging around him, too."

Carolina was right, and it irked him to no end. Natalie was vulnerable. Inexperienced. Susceptible to a man like him.

"We should put a stop to it."

"There's not much we can do." Carolina shrugged. "They're both consenting adults."

"She's our employee."

"But that doesn't give us the right to dictate who she sees and doesn't see."

"I think it does." An idea occurred to Jake. "We could modify our employee contract. Have it state that employees aren't allowed to fraternize with members of the family trust. We already have a no-fraternizing-with-the-guests clause."

"We'd need a family vote for that."

"No, we wouldn't." Jake was liking his idea more and more. So much, in fact, he'd forgotten about his pain. "I have the authority to make the change."

"You're nuts!" Carolina exclaimed. "Natalie will be livid, and rightfully so."

"If it prevents her from making another mistake, I'll take my chances."

"Oh, please," she scoffed. "I don't believe for one second your priority is to spare Natalie heartache. And neither will she."

"I don't care as long as it keeps them apart."

"Well, maybe you should care. Natalie's not the meek little mouse you think she is. Her loyalty to you, to us, has a limit. Your plan to keep them apart might work, but it's just as likely we'll lose one of our best employees. Not to mention a good friend. And what about her parents? We need Gary."

"Natalie won't leave the ranch."

"You said the same thing about Hailey."

Jake didn't appreciate the reminder. He grunted sharply when they rounded a hairpin curve, and Carolina tapped the brakes. "Hey, watch it." He felt as if he was being dragged by the ankle over a bed of sharp rocks.

"Sorry." His cousin's apology had all the sincerity of a used-car salesman's pitch.

"You did that on purpose."

"Who, me?" she asked innocently, then broke into a truly devilish grin.

AARON STOPPED at the reception counter and waited for Natalie to return a file folder to the cabinet drawer. When she turned slowly around, he smiled broadly. Damned if she wasn't pretty. He almost told her so then thought better of it.

"Hey, how's it going?" he asked instead.

"Okay. Jake's waiting for you."

She didn't smile back. Not a real smile. He got one of those fake responses reserved for guests who are annoying but must be tolerated.

Hmm. What had changed between last night at dinner and today? Couldn't be the insurance inspector. He'd had nothing to do with that except show the man around the ranch.

Jake must have gotten to her again.

Aaron make a conscious effort to defuse his anger. As much as he'd like to tell his former brother-in-law where to go, doing so would only worsen things for Natalie, and he didn't want that. Maybe he should follow her cue and back off their friendship for a while.

Yeah, right. Who was he kidding? Their friendship was fast moving into a stage he wasn't quite ready to explore.

"See you later, then."

He circumvented her work area and headed to Jake's office. This wasn't the time or place to confront her with questions he himself couldn't answer or feelings he shouldn't be having. And unless he wanted to make life difficult for her, there might never be a good time or place.

He knocked on the door and entered without waiting for a response.

Jake laid aside the catalog he'd been reading and motioned Aaron in. "Tell me about the visit from the inspector," he began without preamble.

Aaron shut the door behind him and sat in the same chair

he occupied the first day he'd arrived at the ranch. Was it only a week and a half ago? It seemed so much longer than that.

"Everything went well, I think. Real nice guy." He was suddenly distracted by Jake's appearance. "Are you okay?"

"Fine."

"You sure?" Aaron studied him closely. "Because you don't look good."

Jake's forehead glistened with a thin film of perspiration, and he moved as if his joints were fused together. His eyes, so much like Hailey's in shape and appearance, were slightly unfocused and bloodshot.

"I'm fine," he repeated and wiped a hand across his forehead. "Where did you take the inspector? What did the two of you do?"

Aaron decided it was just like Jake to come to work when he was sick. Control freaks refused to relinquish the reins without a fight. How it must gall him that Aaron was recruited to escort the inspector around the ranch because Jake happened to be gone.

"We toured a couple of the guest cabins. Then I took him down to the stables. He also wanted to see the garage and the ATVs and to drive one of the trails." Aaron spent five minutes filling Jake in on all the details. "The guy said we'd get a copy of the report in a week or two."

"Did he mention a reason for the inspection?" Jake, who'd jotted notes all while Aaron talked, wiped again at his brow.

"Are you sure you're okay?" Aaron asked.

Jake's face, already pasty to begin with, turned stark white, and his right hand shook. "Quit asking," he grumbled, proving to Aaron that whatever ailment the man wanted to hide was seriously kicking him in the butt.

So much for being a Good Samaritan, he thought. If Jake preferred to suffer, let him. "He mentioned his office receiving a phone call," Aaron said, addressing Jake's question about the inspector's visit.

"Did you place that phone call?"

Aaron chuckled, which wasn't the reaction Jake expected, given the height at which his eyebrows jumped. "What would I have to gain by calling the insurance company?"

"Making life difficult for me?"

"If the shoe fits, I guess."

"Meaning what?"

"Meaning I'm not you, and orchestrating problems for people who irk me isn't my style." Aaron hadn't intended to speak sharply, but his temper, so easily riled at times, got the better of him. "Think about it, Jake. I'd be an idiot to bite the hand that feeds me."

"So this *is* about the money." He shook his head in disgust. "I knew that's why you came back."

"Hell, yes, it's about the money." Aaron's fingers gripped the chair's armrest and squeezed. "How else do you think I fund the foundation?"

"You expect me to believe you're using the money from the family trust exclusively for good works?"

"I'll have a copy of the foundation's financial statement e-mailed to you today. It lists the different sources of income, all contributions and where they come from. Since you know exactly how much the trust pays me, you'll be able to verify that every dime goes into the foundation."

At first, Aaron thought Jake was taken aback by his outburst. He quickly realized his former brother-in-law was in severe discomfort, and his anger cooled.

"Hey." He started to rise. "Maybe you should lie down for a while."

Jake held up a restraining hand. "I'm fine."

"How many times you going to say that?"

His question earned him a scowl.

Maybe because Jake was in such bad shape Aaron cut him some slack and said in a calmer voice, "I didn't call the insurance company, and I only agreed to take the inspector around because he insisted. I didn't say anything to him that would reflect badly on the ranch, you or the family members. I wouldn't. Hailey cared too much about you and this place for me to sabotage it."

Jake appeared to have gained back some of his strength during Aaron's short speech. "I don't trust you."

"I appreciate the honesty." Aaron smiled. He pushed out of his chair and made for the door. "And just so you know, the feeling's mutual."

"Come back here," Jake demanded. "I'm not through talking to you."

Aaron swung around, his hand resting on the doorknob. "Why don't you admit what's really bothering you?"

Jake wobbled to his feet and braced his hands on his desk. Anger burned in his eyes, along with something else. Guilt possibly?

"You took Hailey away from me. I didn't see her once the last six months of her life."

"And that's my fault?"

"Yes." Jake's breathing had become labored.

Good. Aaron hoped he was hurting bad. "She called, wanting to come home. You told her not to bring me. What the hell kind of brother says that to his sister?"

"One trying to protect her from making the biggest mistake of her life."

"Marrying Hailey wasn't a mistake." All the anger he'd worked so hard to control erupted in a rush. One second more of this and he'd tear into Jake, sick or not. Yanking the door open, he said, "I didn't take Hailey away from here or stop her from coming back. The only person to blame for that is you."

Jake's retort, if he even made one, was muffled by the abruptly closed door and the pounding of Aaron's boots across the floor.

"WHAT THE HECK was that all about?" Millie asked, watching Aaron stride across the lobby and out the door.

"Not sure exactly," Natalie mumbled. She also watched Aaron but more discreetly. "Something to do with the insurance inspector."

"Yeah, right." Millie snorted. "And just yesterday I had a customer bring an undiscovered Picasso into the store."

Natalie gave Jake's aunt a weak smile, her only comment on the situation. The last part of the exchange between him and Aaron had been loud and heated. Everyone within earshot knew it was about Hailey.

"Okay. Let me rephrase that." Millie leaned her elbows on the reception counter and said with exaggerated excitement, "Wow, wasn't that something?"

"You're terrible." Natalie laughed and got out of her chair. She hadn't moved during the entire argument, feeling guilty and thinking she'd somehow contributed by more or less snubbing Aaron.

"When you get to be my age, you don't have to act appropriately anymore." Millie's grin was absolutely inappropriate for the circumstances and impossible to resist.

The door to Alice's office opened slowly, and she peeked out.

"All clear," Millie said in her booming voice. "You don't have to hide anymore."

Alice made a face as if insulted. Throwing back her head, she walked briskly toward them. "I thought you were at the store today, Millie."

"Deana's there. I came to watch the fireworks."

Natalie averted her gaze so no one saw her smirk. Only Jake's aunt could get away with such outrageous behavior.

"Seriously," Alice asked.

"No." Millie chuckled. "I'm meeting the Brubaker bride and her mother in fifteen minutes. They're changing the reception menu again."

"Do you think someone should check on him?" Alice whispered, staring at Jake's closed office door. "He did have outpatient surgery this morning." If she knew the nature of his procedure, she wasn't telling.

"Maybe." Natalie suffered a second twinge of guilt. Jake had looked terrible when he came in a short while ago. She stared imploringly at Millie.

"Hey, leave me out of this."

"You're his aunt," Alice argued.

"You're his assistant."

Both women turned to Natalie.

"No!" she protested in a loud whisper.

"You've known him longer than me," Alice said.

"Millie's known him his whole life."

"I'm a spectator, not a participant." Her wide grin had lost none of its impishness. "And he likes you better than either us."

Alice's I've-just-been-insulted face reappeared.

"What's wrong with my darling nephew anyway?" Millie asked.

Natalie shook her head. "Some kind of medical procedure."

"Spill," Millie demanded of Alice.

"I don't know. Carolina wouldn't say when I spoke to her earlier."

"I'll hit her up later. She can't keep a secret if her life depended on it."

Alice frowned. "I get the feeling Jake doesn't want anyone to know about it."

"When did that ever matter?" Millie pointed at Jake's door. "Go," she told Natalie. "See what you can find out."

Having seven bosses had its disadvantages.

"I'll check on him," she said firmly, "but that's all. Whatever procedure he had done this morning really isn't our concern."

"Killjoy," Millie called after her retreating back.

Natalie knocked softly on Jake's office door.

"Come in."

He sat at his desk, his shoulders stooped, his hair a bit rumpled, as if he'd been holding his head. Ever since Aaron's arrival at the ranch, Jake's well-groomed appearance had gone to the dogs.

"I'm heading over to the dining hall for some coffee," she began. "You want me to bring you back anything?"

"No, thanks." He didn't glance up or acknowledge her in any way.

"Sure?"

"You've done your job, you've checked on me. I'm all right." His tone wasn't angry as much as weary. "Now, leave me alone if you don't mind."

Natalie ducked out and shut the door, feeling guiltier than before. He must know people were talking about him. She was also concerned. Jake might not be the easiest person to get along with at times, but he'd always been good to her and her family.

"Well?" Millie demanded. She and Alice hadn't moved from their respective spots.

"He says he's okay."

Alice's hopeful expression fell. "I think he's lying."

"Of course he's lying." Millie dismissed Alice's worry with an airy wave. "He's Jake. Prideful, arrogant and stubborn." Her voiced warmed. "Gotta love him."

Alice fidgeted, wringing her hands like a distraught mother. "I don't know what to do. We have all these last-minute details to take care of before the opening-day celebration. Should I go in there or leave him alone?"

Jake's office door unexpectedly opened. With a cursory nod toward the three women, he walked by, slow yet erect, and exited through the front door.

"Great," Alice wailed and dashed to the window. "Where's he going?"

Millie resumed resting her elbows on the counter. "If I were you, I'd quit panicking about those last-minute things. He isn't coming back."

With a frustrated groan, Alice dropped the curtain, spun on her heels and retreated to her office.

"What got into her?" Millie muttered.

"This has been the craziest day." Natalie pushed her hair out of her face and sighed. With all the various disruptions of the last few hours, she'd almost forgotten about the letter from Drew's attorney and that not one person had returned the phone calls she'd placed during lunch.

"I'll say." Millie also sighed, but hers was pleasurable rather than woeful, and her eyes danced with delight. "Am I the only one who thinks opening-day celebration this year is going to be the best ever?"

Chapter Seven

Each time the lobby door opened to let people in or out, the smell of simmering chili wafted inside. After three hours, Natalie was ravenous, and she didn't even like chili all that much.

When her replacement arrived at three-thirty, Natalie loaded Shiloh in her stroller and headed outside. Because of the informality of the day, Jake had allowed Natalie to keep her daughter with her, for which she was appreciative. Leaving Shiloh in someone else's care while she went to work was hard.

Yesterday, the family-trust attorney finally returned her phone calls and gave her the name of another attorney specializing in child-custody matters. She had an appointment on Wednesday next week. The attorney strongly urged Natalie to wait before agreeing to Drew's request until she was fully informed of all the ramifications.

Natalie stopped for a moment to get her bearings. Opening-day celebration was still going strong and by the looks of things, promised to continue long past dinner. Jake was sure to be pleased. The good news might lift him out of his sour mood.

At the foot of the stone walkway, Natalie veered left to the area designated for the chili cook-off. It was a little strange seeing the ranch overrun with people after almost seven weeks of solitude. Over two hundred people were on the grounds and probably a hundred more had come and gone throughout the afternoon.

Dinner would be served following the horseshoe tournament. After that was the awards ceremony. Natalie's mother usually handed out the plaques to the various winners. This year, Natalie would do it while her mother sat in the audience with Shiloh.

Folding tables had been set up for the cook-off contestants with two entries per table. The ranch had also provided single-burner butane cookstoves. Everything else, from kettles to ingredients, was left up to the contestants.

Natalie had no idea where or how Aaron had acquired everything he'd needed to make his chili but there he was, at the second to the last table, stirring a huge pot and chatting companionably with his tablemate.

She didn't immediately hurry over, though she longed to do just that. Except for a periodic glimpse of him in the distance, she hadn't seen Aaron since the other day when he left Jake's office. *Stormed* from Jake's office, she corrected herself.

Not talking to Aaron proved more difficult than she'd imagined. It wasn't just that she liked him, which she definitely did. More than she should. Her heart also went out to him. Coming to Bear Creek Ranch couldn't be easy for him, and except for Millie, the Tucker family was doing their best to throw barriers in his path every step of the way.

If they'd only stop and get to know him a little, they'd see he wasn't such a bad guy. And though her father hadn't come right out and said it, Natalie was sure he liked and respected Aaron, too. For his horsemanship abilities and his ease with people. The guests, her father recently commented, would love him.

She stopped and checked on Shiloh—who preferred sucking on her balled fist to watching the goings-on—before joining the group in front of the first table.

Their celebrity judge, Dan "Quick Draw" McGraw, was a

popular afternoon DJ from Payson's largest radio station. He laughed heartily as he interviewed the contestants. Shadowing him were a pair of techies who lugged equipment and handed Quick Draw the microphone at the appropriate time.

One contestant fidgeted during the entire interview and accidentally spilled her chili sample on Quick Draw's arm. He used the incident to make several jokes to the on-air and live audiences. The red-faced contestant giggled right along with everybody else.

Like spectators in a golf tournament, the crowd moved from table to table. Natalie tagged along. She was curious to see how Aaron fared and by blending in with the crowd, no one would think twice.

No one being Jake.

Quick Draw did a double take when he approached Aaron's table and made a show of reading the name tag and entry number pinned to his shirt pocket.

"Aaron Reyes? As in three-time national bronc-riding champion?"

Aaron's tablemate's jaw dropped open. "You didn't tell me that."

"It's been a couple of years," he said, stirring his chili.

"Nice to meet you, sir." Quick Draw stuck out his hand, which Aaron shook. "Mind if I ask what brings you to these parts?" With his other hand, he motioned for the techie holding the microphone.

"My mother's chili recipe."

Quick Draw looked unsure for a moment, then broke into a hearty belly laugh. "That good, huh?"

"You tell me." Aaron ladled a portion into a paper bowl and gave it to Quick Draw.

"Going to the Payson Rodeo week after next?" he asked.

"I was thinking of stopping by. Checking on a few old friends."

The rodeo was a huge annual event that drew thousands of people, both tourists and participants, to town. Natalie had two dozen cabins reserved already for that week and expected to be booked solid.

Quick Draw sampled Aaron's chili, and his face lit up. "Not bad." He waved the techie with the microphone closer. "What's your secret ingredient?"

"Don't have one."

"No?" Quick Draw's gesture encompassed the entire area. "Everyone else here does."

"It's not what goes into the chili as much as the preparation involved. The trick is adding the right ingredients in the right amounts at the right time." Aaron's voice deepened, and for the first time, Natalie detected a slight accent. "Don't hurry. Cooking is a slow, intricate process and should be executed with care and finesse."

She hadn't thought he noticed her among the crowd, but when his gaze sought hers and lingered, she realized he'd been aware of her from the beginning, and a jolt went through her.

"You almost sound like you're seducing a woman," Quick Draw said, taking another bite of chili, "and not cooking."

"The two aren't all that different."

Natalie was affected by his voice and his eyes, which were not just looking at her but inside her to that part she revealed to only a few. They might have been sharing a candlelight dinner in a quiet restaurant, both of them wondering if the evening was going to end with a kiss on her doorstep.

Thank goodness Natalie had the stroller to hang on to, because her knees went weak. Even Drew, the first and only man she'd ever slept with, hadn't evoked such a response in her.

"Well," Quick Draw bellowed. "I don't know if you've made the best chili here, but you sure as hell gave the best description of your cooking process." He looked over his shoulder at the crowd. "What do you think, ladies?"

He was answered by applause and cheers.

Aaron's attention returned to the DJ. Except for Natalie's buttery knees and burning cheeks, the entire exchange might not have happened.

She lowered her head so no one would notice her acute embarrassment. What was wrong with her? Not once but twice now she'd assumed Aaron was coming on to her when he was just being…Aaron. Naturally friendly. Naturally sexy. Naturally flirtatious in that slow, easy way of his.

She needed to quit letting her desire for him cloud her judgment.

Desire! Had she really just thought that?

Yes, and it was true. She did desire Aaron. And not in a schoolgirl-crush way either but like a woman who's finally met the man she's been waiting for her whole life.

She decided to leave and find her mother and the plaques, but with so many people behind her, she couldn't back up the stroller and get away. Trapped, she was forced to watch Quick Draw finish his interview with Aaron.

"Well, this has been a real pleasure, sir. Good luck with the cook-off."

"Thank you. I'll be sure and let my mother know what you think of her recipe."

Aaron had handled himself well during the interview, conversing comfortably with the DJ as if they were old friends. Natalie supposed he was no stranger to the media. And he had cohosted that cable rodeo show.

"I'm probably speaking out of turn here," Quick Draw said, "but I'm sure our producer won't mind. Any chance I can get you to come by the station's booth at the rodeo next week? We'd love to have you do a spot with us. Maybe give a little color commentary on the contestants."

"Sure. Sounds like fun."

Quick Draw beamed. "We'll see you then." Handing the microphone back to the techie, he said to Aaron, "Let's talk after the dinner," in a much more serious voice, then moved on to the next table.

Natalie tried to turn the stroller to the right, but the front wheel was caught on something and refused to budge. When jiggling the stroller didn't free the wheel, she knelt for a closer look. Shiloh perked up and started gurgling.

"Hey, sweetie. How are you doing?"

The crowd moved ahead, leaving them behind. Natalie discovered a small rock wedged between the wheel and a bottom rod. It took several seconds to dislodge it.

"There." She tossed it aside.

Shiloh's gurgling grew louder, and her eyes widened.

"I'm happy, too." Natalie stood…and discovered Aaron had come around from the table. She nearly knocked him over. "Oh!"

"Everything okay?"

"Just a rock caught in the wheel." Her heart skipped. She hadn't been this close to him since that day on the porch when he'd quieted Shiloh's crying with a lullaby. "I, uh, got it."

He tipped his head in the direction of Quick Draw. "Better hurry if you want to catch up."

"Yeah." Only she wasn't hurrying. The sparks in his eyes interfered with her brain's ability to control her limbs.

Sparks? Yes, definitely. And aimed at her.

Natalie let out a long, slow and quite uneven breath. What, if anything, should she do now?

THE HORSESHOE SAILED through the air and landed in the dirt with one prong touching the stake. Spectators whooped and clapped.

"Where'd you learn to pitch like that?" Aaron asked Skunk.

He shrugged and held up two fingers to the scorekeeper sitting in a lawn chair on the sidelines.

One thing about Skunk; he'd perfected the art of silent communication. Aaron couldn't recall him saying one word in their entire three-week acquaintance.

They stepped back from the horseshoe pit and watched the first of their two opponents pitch. The horseshoe landed too far from the stake to count. Good. Aaron and Skunk were ahead but only by a point. They couldn't make any mistakes in the next few pitches or they'd risk losing.

Aaron bent and retrieved the horseshoe from the ground in front of him. Hefting it in his hand until the weight felt comfortable, he took his position behind the line. From the corner of his eye, he spotted Natalie. She stood at the edge of the crowd, arms resting on the stroller handle and watching him. Just like she'd watched him during the chili cook-off. He'd watched her, too. Every second his mind wasn't otherwise occupied. Which reminded him…

Swinging his arm back and forth, Aaron took careful aim. The horseshoe connected with the stake, spun twice and fell into the dirt. Aaron grinned. That was his best shot of the tournament, bar none.

"Foul," Jake hollered from the sidelines and slashed the air with his hand. "You stepped outside the pitching pad."

"No way!" It was one of the spectators who objected, not Aaron. The rowdy fan was joined by several of his buddies. "His feet never moved."

"No score," Jake reiterated.

Skunk's angry scowl demanded to know if Aaron was going to take that bogus call lying down.

"He's the judge." Aaron learned long ago not to dispute officials no matter how angry he got. It hadn't gained him anything in the rodeo ring and wouldn't here today either. "We can still win this."

Jake was judging the team horseshoe tournament only because he'd lost the singles one. The winner was a seventeen-year-old girl from Phoenix whose low-waisted shorts and skimpy top revealed a jeweled belly-button ring. Aaron didn't blame Jake for taking the loss hard. He would have, too. But dang if the girl didn't pitch a mean game of horseshoes.

Aaron and Skunk's opponent took his turn. The crowd increased in size during the last minutes. With the score tied going into the final inning, tension mounted. Skunk threw a ringer just when he and Aaron needed it the most. Teresa called out to him, and Skunk surprised Aaron by smiling shyly.

Their opponents crumbled under the pressure. One overshot his pitch, the other undershot his. Which was fortunate because Aaron didn't pitch so well himself. It was enough, however, to win them the tournament. Their opponents came over to offer their congratulations.

Jake slipped away. It was then Aaron happened to notice Jake's former wife, Ellen, among the crowd. She clung to the arm of a man Aaron didn't recognize. For the first time ever, he felt a little sorry for Jake.

Teresa burst through the cheering crowd and charged them, shouting, "You won, you won." At nearly six feet tall, she was a sight to behold and not a little intimidating. Reaching them, she picked up Skunk, who weighed a good thirty pounds less than her, and squeezed him to her. "Boy, you were seriously hot out there."

"Wanna have supper with me?" he asked when she put him down.

"Hell, yes!"

Aaron stared in amazement, not sure which stunned him more. Skunk uttering an entire sentence or his and Teresa's apparent budding romance.

"Congratulations." Natalie stood behind him. He'd been too preoccupied to noticed her approach.

"Thanks," he murmured, momentarily at a loss for words. Late-afternoon sunlight glinted off her blond curls and turned her blue eyes a striking shade of aqua. Perhaps because of the guests visiting the ranch, she'd dressed up. Slim-fitting black pants took the place of baggy blue jeans, and the rounded neckline of her embroidered blouse revealed a smooth expanse of freckle-kissed skin.

"Want to have dinner with me?" He spoke without thinking. Well, the line had worked for Skunk.

"I…um…can't." She hesitated then admitted, "Jake invited me to sit with him and Quick Draw McGraw. And since I'm handing out the plaques…" She didn't finish her sentence.

"Another time maybe?"

"Absolutely." She pushed the stroller ahead a couple of feet then stopped. "I'll see you at the awards ceremony." The smile she flashed him was warm and bright and so incredibly sweet. Not the one she reserved for guests.

Aaron felt a sharp pain in his chest. He didn't worry, for he knew what caused it. After two years of near inactivity, his damaged heart was beating strong again.

EVEN THOUGH NATALIE declined Aaron's dinner invitation, he wound up eating with her after all. It was Quick Draw who'd insisted and then monopolized most of the conversation. He was apparently quite serious about Aaron joining the KRDS Radio team during their three-day live broadcast from the Payson Rodeo. And Aaron was apparently quite serious about joining them.

Jake sat quietly during most of dinner. Natalie was probably the only one at the table who knew the real reason for his silence, which had nothing to do with Aaron, a slip of a girl breaking his four-year winning streak at horseshoes, or the ranch. His ex-wife had unexpectedly shown up at the opening-day celebration with her new boyfriend. And though Jake pretended differently, he was suffering.

He and Natalie excused themselves before dessert was served in order to get ready for the awards ceremony. Alice helped Natalie set up the podium and microphone. Within minutes, they were ready. While Jake gave a small speech, Natalie conducted a last-minute check on the plaques she and her mother had made.

Her hand paused briefly on the one for Aaron. She was glad he'd won the team-horseshoe tournament. Jake had been wrong to call that one shot of Aaron's a foul. Wrong to take his anger at his ex-wife, understandable as it may be, out on Aaron.

At the end of his short speech, Jake motioned for Natalie to bring the plaques and called Quick Draw up to the podium to announce the winner of the chili cook-off.

"Whooo, wheee," Quick Draw said into the microphone, his clownish grin stretching from ear to ear. "We sure have tasted some mighty fine chili today. Haven't we, folks?"

Applause for the contestants followed.

While the DJ joked for several minutes, imparting some of

the more amusing anecdotes from the taste testing that afternoon, Carolina snapped pictures. One or two were bound to wind up in the photo albums kept at Founders Cabin.

"Well, let's end the suspense, shall we?" Quick Draw said. "And announce the winner." He pulled a tiny slip of paper from his shirt pocket and unfolded it. "I'm probably going to butcher this name so please excuse me."

Natalie knew then Aaron hadn't won, and her eyes sought his. He obviously knew, too, from the look on his face, though he didn't appear upset or disappointed. He clapped enthusiastically when Quick Draw called the winner's name. As promised, he butchered it.

The woman who won gave a little gasp when she leaped from her seat and dashed up the center aisle to collect her plaque. She hugged Quick Draw and Natalie and gushed when she shared the secret of her recipe with the audience.

Quick Draw resumed his seat, and Jake took over. There were eight awards in total, and the presentations went quickly. Jake was decent to the young girl who bested him at horseshoes, shaking her hand and complimenting her on her game. But when someone from the back of the room ribbed him, his smiled thinned.

The last award was for team horseshoes.

"And the winners are Skunk Studemeyer and Aaron Reyes."

"Yeah, baby." Teresa cheered wildly from her table. "You rock."

Natalie had seen some interesting romances between coworkers during her years at the ranch. Skunk and Teresa's rated as one of the more unexpected ones.

He collected his plaque first. "Good going, Skunk," Natalie told him.

A grunt and curt nod were his only reply. He didn't appear to want a hug, so she didn't offer him one.

Aaron was a different matter. She no sooner handed him his plaque than he swooped her up in his arms.

Natalie's breath caught. Held.

Lack of oxygen must have affected her brain, for she did the unthinkable. She looped her arms around his neck. His hold tightened ever so slightly. One hand came to rest on the small of her back.

"Let go of her," Jake said, his voice low and lethal.

Natalie instantly stiffened and tried to pull away.

Aaron wouldn't let her go.

"Reyes," Jake warned, his tone forceful. He'd stepped away from the podium and had his back to the tables.

She withdrew far enough to look into Aaron's face. His eyes were so dark they appeared almost black. Another time, under different circumstances, she'd have gotten lost in their depths. "Please."

"For you," he whispered and released her. "Not him."

Natalie was glad he cooperated. She didn't want to give Jake another reason to dislike Aaron.

Though it seemed much longer, the whole incident had probably taken a mere ten or fifteen seconds. Mustering her courage, she glanced at the audience. A few people stared at them with any curiosity. Among them were her father, Millie, Carolina and Skunk, who still stood to the side of the podium.

Great.

Aaron and Skunk returned to their seats. Jake closed the awards ceremony with an invitation for everyone to return to the ranch another day and enjoy the new amenities. He wore his game face and acted as if nothing was the matter. Not that she'd have expected anything else from him.

"Everyone stay. There's plenty of dessert and coffee left over," he announced before leaving the podium to visit with the remaining guests.

Natalie avoided Aaron. If her presence weren't mandatory, she'd collect Shiloh from her mother and go home. She also avoided Jake. Not because she feared talking to him. If he did say anything to her about Aaron's hug, it wouldn't be here or tonight. But he had a way of making a person feel three inches tall with just a look, and she had no wish to be on the receiving end of that look. Not until she had a chance to figure out what exactly transpired between her and Aaron and what she intended to do about it.

Nightfall had come and gone by the time the last guest left the dining hall. The kitchen crew emerged in full force to finish cleaning and rearrange the tables. Natalie's parents helped pack away the few items remaining from the awards ceremony then decided to head home with Shiloh. Jake had also left sometime earlier. Aaron before him.

Alice said little while she worked. She either hadn't observed the subtle goings between Natalie and Aaron or was too tired to care.

"You did a good job," Natalie told her when they were done with everything. "The chili cook-off was a real success."

"Thanks." Alice's smile, though weary, was friendly.

Natalie decided her coworker wasn't so bad after all. "I'll finish up. Why don't you call it quits."

"You don't mind?"

"Get out of here."

A minute later, Natalie was alone. Ten minutes later, she'd carted the last box to the storage closet and was heading out the door. Cool, crisp air greeted her as she walked onto the porch, and she fastened the top button on her jacket. At the top of the steps, a voice stopped her.

It was Aaron's. He stood by a wicker rocker. "Can I walk you home?"

"Ah…that's all right. I have the golf cart. But thank you anyway."

He took a step toward her. "Then maybe you can give me a ride home."

Natalie's gaze traveled to his arms. She remembered the sensation of them closing around her, how strong they were, how nice they felt.

"I…um…" When had she become a tongue-tied teenager? Pulling herself together, she said, "Sure," with only a faint trace of breathlessness. She could hardly say no. He was one of the owners.

"Leave her the hell alone!"

Natalie spun around at the unexpected intrusion.

Jake stood at the foot of the porch steps, his form a black silhouette against the distant glow from the parking-lot lights.

Chapter Eight

"You heard me, Reyes," Jake said, climbing the porch steps two at a time. "Leave Natalie alone."

"In the first place, I'm not bothering her." Aaron emerged from beneath the shadows cast by the overhanging eaves. "In the second place, you're not in charge of her. Not where I'm concerned."

Natalie felt as if she were standing in the middle of a lonely railroad track with two locomotives approaching from opposite directions. A crash was inevitable and if she didn't do something quickly, she'd be at the center of it.

"Why don't I drop the both of you off." Wrong thing to say. The instant the words were out, Natalie wished she could retract them. Jake had stopped living on the ranch a while ago, something she frequently forgot. He obviously didn't appreciate the reminder. "At your car," she amended.

"No, thanks." He came onto the porch and into the light. Gone was the game face from earlier. He was furious and anyone looking at him would know it. "I'll take you home. Reyes can walk."

"And leave her without transportation in the morning?" Aaron reclined against the porch railing and hooked his thumbs in the front pockets of his jeans. "That's not very fair of you." His casual stance fooled no one. Beneath his calm exterior, a raging storm brewed.

"Jake, I'm sorry," Natalie said. The locomotives were gaining speed, and she had yet to get off the tracks. "It was my fault. I gave all the win—"

"Why are you apologizing?" Aaron demanded. "You didn't do anything wrong."

"No, *you* did." Jake leveled a finger at him.

Natalie supposed she should be grateful it wasn't a fist.

"Exactly what did I do?" Aaron unhooked his thumbs. His eyes never left Jake.

"You had your hands all over her."

"I hugged her."

"You practically molested her in front of everyone there." Jake advanced.

"He didn't," Natalie pleaded. "Really."

Jake stopped short, shook his head and laughed bitterly. "I can't believe you're defending him."

"Nothing happened." And nothing had. Except in her over-active imagination.

"If I didn't know better," Aaron said, "I'd think you were jealous."

Jake's stare went from ice cold to red hot. "Natalie is an employee of this ranch. I don't have personal relationships with the employees. I recommend you adhere to the same practice."

She shouldn't let what he said hurt her. But it did. She'd always considered herself a friend. Not just another one of the workers, the majority of whom came and went with each new season.

She caught Aaron studying her and quickly turned away.

"You're an even bigger fool than I thought," he told Jake. "Hailey was right about you."

Jake let loose a ripe expletive and started toward Aaron. "Don't you dare bring my sister into this!"

In response, Aaron pushed off the column and came at Jake. "I'll bring my wife into it any damn time I please."

Scant seconds separated the locomotives from their impending collision. Natalie had only one chance to avert certain disaster. Putting herself directly between the two men, she held up her hands and shouted, "Enough!"

They obediently halted. Surprise showed in Jake's eyes. Respect in Aaron's.

She released the breath that had lodged in her throat. Raising her voice wasn't something Natalie did and certainly not to her boss.

"I have never had an inappropriate relationship with anyone on this ranch," she said, feeling less in control than she sounded. "Family members or otherwise. And just to set the record straight—" her gaze alternated between Aaron and Jake "—I don't intend to."

Neither had a comeback, which suited her just fine because she was pretty much fed up with both of them.

"See you in the morning." She pushed past Jake and trotted down the steps. "You can have the golf cart." She didn't tell them what they could do with it. "I'll walk home."

Nothing like a mile-long hike in the chilly night air to take the edge off a person's temper. It occurred to her only after she reached the stone walkway that she'd just mouthed off to her boss. According to the company manual, insubordination was grounds for termination.

Tomorrow was *so* not going to be a good day at work.

Instead of taking the main road, she cut through the parking lot, crossed a grassy knoll and scampered down one of the guest trails leading to Bear Creek.

A three-quarter moon rising over the distant mountaintops provided enough light for her to see. Beside her, the creek gurgled and splashed, its glassy surface reflecting the million and one stars in the sky. Overhead, an owl hooted, warning her away from his territory. She hadn't taken this particular shortcut since she was a teenager and had sneaked out of her parents' house to go with Carolina to a party. The well-worn path was smooth beneath her feet and indicated the current generation of Bear Creek Ranch kids was still making use of it.

Natalie stooped and swatted at a low-hanging branch before it struck her in the face. In the near distance, she heard the buzz of the golf cart. Jake taking Aaron home? Not likely. After tonight, she doubted they'd remain in the same room together much less drive the ranch roads side by side in a pint-size vehicle. Aaron must be heading to his bunkhouse alone.

Had Jake not appeared when he did, Natalie would have been the one to drive Aaron home. And what then? Would they have picked up where his hug left off? Jake was wrong *and* right. Wrong because Aaron hadn't practically molested her. Right because their embrace had been more than a platonic hug.

Reaching the end of the shortcut, she scaled a small slope thick with foliage and came out beside the road. There, she stopped to wipe the dirt and bits of dried leaves from her pants. Her cabin lay about twenty yards in the distance. Her parents' cabin, twenty yards beyond that.

Natalie's pace was considerably slower now than it had been on her hike along the creek. No longer furious, she felt sad and empty. For herself—she liked Aaron and wouldn't mind pursuing a relationship with him if circumstances were different—but mostly for him and Jake. They'd both loved Hailey, both grieved her death. Those shared emotions should bring two people closer, not tear them apart.

Distracted by her thoughts, Natalie's foot came down on a large rock, throwing her off balance. She caught herself before she fell but not soon enough to prevent twisting her ankle. Pain shot up her leg. It didn't last. When she tentatively placed weight on her foot, she discovered there was no real damage, except to her pride.

Events of the last week caught up with her in one big emotional rush. The letter from Shiloh's father's attorney. Jake's surgery. The unannounced inspection from the insurance company. Aaron's hug tonight. Her response to it. Jake's reaction to it. And now her stupid ankle.

She promptly and unexpectedly burst into tears.

"Are you okay, Natalie?" Aaron appeared out of nowhere. His hand closed around her arm, his grip firm but solicitous.

"I'm fine." She sniffled, fought without success to stanch the flow of tears. "I tripped."

"Are you hurt?"

"Just embarrassed." She wiped at her nose and eyes with the back of her hand. "What are you doing here?"

"I've been waiting by your cabin." He pointed, and she saw the outline of the golf cart parked next to her car. "Wanted to make sure you got home safe and sound."

That was sweet of him. Jake hadn't stuck around to make sure she'd gotten home safe and sound. But then he knew she was familiar with every inch of this ranch.

"Where'd you go when you took off?" He guided her toward her cabin. "I drove around looking for you."

"An old shortcut." Her attempt to remove her arm from his grasp was met with resistance. "Really. I can walk by myself." Thank goodness she'd finally stopped crying.

"You Forresters. All alike."

"I beg your pardon?"

"Thickheaded and stubborn to boot. Your father drives me crazy. So do you." He turned his head, caught her glance, lowered his voice. "In more ways than one."

If he weren't already supporting her, she might have tripped again.

"Watch yourself," he murmured. They were scaling the first porch step when he unexpectedly pulled her to a halt. "Let's sit a minute."

"Aaron."

Ignoring her protest, he sat on the top step and tugged her down beside him. She was too stunned to refuse.

Her entire left side, from shoulder to knee, touched his entire right side. Not indecent exactly but there was something sensual, so unnervingly provocative about it. Beneath her jacket, she shivered. No, make that trembled. In anticipation.

If she went all melty inside at the brush of his leg, what

would happen if he, say, held her hand? Put an arm around her? Kissed her?

What she ought to do was discourage him. Just so he didn't get any ideas. Though as far as Natalie could tell, she was the only one in the vicinity getting ideas. She should talk about Jake. That would squash any romantic inclinations she had…er, make that, Aaron had.

"You know, Jake isn't always so difficult to get along with. He had a rough day. Personally, that is. Businesswise, we did great."

"You're joking," Aaron said dryly. "He's been difficult to get along with since the day I met him."

"It seems that way to you because you're always getting the brunt of his bad mood."

"Yeah. That would give me reason to think he can't stand the sight of me."

"His ex-wife was at the opening-day celebration today."

"She lives here, doesn't she? With their girls?"

"Yeah. She brought some guy with her."

"I saw them together."

"Then you can understand how that would bother a guy."

"Depends on how the guy feels about his ex-wife."

"Jake didn't want the divorce. Because of the girls. He agreed only on the condition his ex-wife not move off the ranch until their youngest turns eighteen. He gets to see his daughters every day, which is nice. On the downside, he has to watch another man spend time with them. Go on dates with his ex-wife. Eat dinner at his table."

"You're right. It sucks. And would make anybody irritable."

"Exactly!" She sighed, leaning against Aaron as she did. "You understand."

"That Jake's angry at his ex-wife? Sure. At me? No. I had nothing to do with his marriage falling apart."

"Of course you didn't. But look at it from his point of view for a second. He loses his baby sister in an accident. A year later, he catches his wife cheating on him. Reservations drop off, and the ranch has its worst season in history. The man's entitled to be irritable."

Aaron angled his body toward her. The movement, though slight, increased the pressure where their bodies touched. His breath tickled her hair, fanned her cheek, raised goose bumps on arms covered by several thick layers of clothing.

Natalie didn't dare move. One twitch, one jerk, and she'd wind up in Aaron's lap. Her thoughts, spinning already, went off in an entirely new direction.

"Jake's wrong about you," he whispered into her ear.

"He is?" Did her voice really just squeak?

"You're more than an employee. You're his friend. A good one." Aaron lifted a hand and captured her chin, tipping her face up until their eyes met. "And if he doesn't see that, he doesn't deserve you. As a friend *or* an employee."

"If you gave him a chance, you'd—"

Natalie might have continued if Aaron's lips weren't suddenly covering hers. Parting them. Molding them to fit his. His hand slid from her chin to the side of her neck, then to the back of her head where his fingers threaded into the loose curls of her hair. She sank into him because not succumbing was impossible.

Aaron was an expert kisser. Or, maybe it was the secret wanting and wondering of the last three weeks that had every nerve in her body humming with a need unbearable in its intensity.

She could probably stop him with a word or a move. But she didn't. Not when he deepened the kiss and not when his other arm fell to her waist and circled it. The tiny part of her brain still thinking coherently warned her to snap out of it. If she valued her job and her home, she'd stop kissing Aaron and run like the dickens into her cabin.

The rest of her brain, the part thinking incoherently, urged her to enjoy while it lasted.

Soon—too soon—Aaron pulled back. He didn't, however, release her, and she let herself relish the sensation of his arms wrapped snugly around her.

Smiling down at her, he asked, "What are you thinking?"

"That I lied to Jake."

"About what?"

"I told him I'd never have an inappropriate relationship with anyone on this ranch, including family members."

"I don't know." Aaron pressed his lips to her forehead. "This feels pretty appropriate to me."

She couldn't argue with him and neither could she explain. They fit together perfectly and not just on the porch steps. But that, Natalie reminded herself, didn't automatically make having a relationship a good idea. Not when her boss was so adamantly opposed.

"I have to go." She rose in a hurry. "Mom brought Shiloh home from the dinner for me and is waiting up."

Aaron's hand remained briefly on her arm. She half expected him to try to prevent her from leaving.

He didn't.

She squared her shoulders and said, "We can't do this again," trying to sound firm and not as if she was issuing a dare.

He stood. "I won't endanger your job or your friendship with Jake. I promise."

She swallowed and tried to convince herself it was what she wanted. "Thank you. I appreciate that."

"I won't, however, promise not to kiss you again."

Any protest she might have made was thwarted by his fingers caressing her cheek with soft strokes. The next moment, he was gone, walking down the dark road toward his bunkhouse.

Natalie touched her face, which still tingled from his caress. If Aaron was a man of his word, and she highly suspected he was, she would have to guard herself diligently. A girl could only resist the man of her dreams for so long.

"YOU'RE LATE." Natalie's mother sat up in the recliner and blinked the drowsiness from her eyes. "Dad came by—" she checked her watch "—a little past nine."

"I sent Alice home and cleaned up by myself."

Natalie went straight to the small bedroom across the hall. Shiloh slept soundly in her cradle. The soft glow of the night-light combining with a pale pink sleeper gave her baby daughter the appearance of a tiny angel. As she did every day, Natalie mouthed a silent prayer of thanks for the precious miracle that had come into her life.

Drew was an idiot. He had no idea what he was missing by not knowing his daughter. The indecisiveness she'd felt since receiving his letter instantly vanished. Alice and the child-custody attorney were right. Drew should pay. Generously.

If Shiloh was going to be denied a relationship with her father, she should at least have the benefit of his money. Health insurance. A college education. Dance lessons if that was what she wanted. A car when she was old enough to drive. All the extras in life Natalie would have trouble affording on her salary.

She was quite suddenly looking forward to her appointment with the child-custody attorney this coming week.

Leaning down, she kissed her daughter's head and smelled the faint scent of baby shampoo. Somebody must have gotten a bath before bed.

Her mother had turned off the TV and was waiting for Natalie in the kitchen.

"How was she tonight?" Natalie asked.

"Perfect. Sweet as always. Fussed a little at bedtime but only for a few minutes."

"Good."

"So, what did you and Aaron talk about outside for so long?"

Natalie was too thunderstruck to hide her reaction. "How did you know?"

"He came by in the golf cart. Said you were walking home from the dining hall and that he was worried about you. I told him you've walked home from the dining hall a thousand times. He didn't seem assured. When I didn't hear the golf cart leave, I figured he was waiting for you. Am I right?"

"Yes." Natalie removed a glass from the cupboard and

poured herself some iced tea. She wasn't concerned about caffeine this late at night. Remembering Aaron's kiss was going to keep her up till the wee hours of the morning as it was.

"You want to talk about what happened?" Deana asked.

"Outside?" Natalie stopped in midsip. Did her mother suspect she and Aaron had kissed?

"The hug."

"Oh." Almost as bad as the kiss.

"Your dad and I are concerned, honey." Deana helped herself to a glass of iced tea. Apparently she didn't plan on getting to sleep at a decent hour either.

"I'm a big girl, Mom." Natalie bristled. Her mother meant well, but her tone hinted at past mistakes and that Natalie didn't always make the best decisions where men were concerned. "I can take care of myself."

"We're not trying to interfere in your life or tell you what to do. Merely letting you know we're here if you need us."

Natalie nodded. The iced tea didn't taste as good as she thought it would, and she set the glass down on the counter.

"Aaron's a terrific guy," her mother went on. "Don't get me wrong. Your dad and I both like him."

Natalie waited for the "but" that was sure to follow.

"But besides being a member of the family trust, he has a lot of unresolved issues where Hailey is concerned."

"You and Dad comparing notes again?"

Deana didn't respond to the sharp bite in Natalie's voice. "He and your father have talked some. Not so much about Hailey."

"Then how do you know he has unresolved issues?" It occurred to Natalie she was being intentionally obtuse. No one ever entirely got over the death of a spouse.

"It's pretty obvious, don't you think? Him coming to the ranch. The foundation. His bitterness toward Jake."

"Aaron's bitterness toward Jake isn't without cause. He forbid Hailey to bring Aaron here after they were married and has treated him horribly since the day he arrived."

"You're right." Deana finished the last of her iced tea and rinsed out the glass. "Has it occurred to you Aaron's reasons for getting close to you might not be aboveboard?"

"Meaning?"

"He could be using you to get back at Jake."

"That's ridiculous," Natalie protested vehemently. Aaron's kiss wasn't faked. She'd stake her heart on it. "He's not a deceitful person."

"Are you sure?" Deana scrutinized her closely. "The truth is, we only met him a few weeks ago."

"You don't have to be acquainted with someone for years to know they're a good and honest person." Aaron had quieted her crying baby by singing her a lullaby. Deceitful people didn't sing lullabies to babies.

"Your dad and I just want you to be cautious. You're vulnerable right now."

"It's been almost a year since Drew left. I'm over him, Mom."

"That's good to hear. You were quite sad there for a while after he…"

"Dumped me. It's okay. You can say it."

"I was thinking abandoned you."

Natalie closed her eyes and rubbed her suddenly throbbing temples. Caustic comments only served to support her mother's belief she was acting impulsively, rather than dispute it.

"Trust me. There's nothing you've said tonight I haven't already thought of."

"What about the fact that Aaron's leaving Bear Creek Ranch in five weeks when his stint is over? Have you thought about that?"

Natalie's stomach dropped to her knees. She didn't reply for several seconds, would have avoided replying altogether if her mother weren't standing there, silently demanding an answer.

"No," she finally muttered. "I haven't."

Chapter Nine

The horse sprang into the air, neck bowed, back bent nearly in half and front hooves a good three feet off the ground. It was almost enough to unseat his rider.

A young cowboy who'd started rodeoing about the same time Aaron retired hung on to the hack rein. His legs were extended so high over the horse's head, he looked as if he was lying down on the saddle rather than sitting in it. At precisely seven point two seconds, the horse—aptly named Red Rocket—launched the cowboy into an orbit that ended with his face planted in the dirt. He rolled onto his back but didn't immediately rise.

One of the pickup men spurred his mount into a gallop and raced toward the fallen cowboy. The other two went after the wildly bucking horse and herded him out of the arena.

"Let's hear it for this young man," the announcer said over the loudspeaker. "What do you say, folks?"

The crowd responded with applause and cheers.

His gut in a knot, Aaron waited along with two thousand spectators at the Payson Rodeo for the cowboy to get up. He relaxed only when the cowboy staggered to his feet with the help of the pickup man, the wind knocked out of him but otherwise in one piece.

Hat in hand, he waved to the crowd, then limped toward the gate. Unfortunately, he'd have nothing but aches and pains to show for his efforts today. The winnings would go to another competitor who'd lasted the full eight seconds and given the judges a good show to boot. Saddle bronc riding was more than a timed event. Scores were also based on the rider's style and the horse's bucking ability. Even if this cowboy hadn't been thrown eight-tenths of a second before the buzzer sounded, chances were he wouldn't have placed.

Oh, well. Better luck next time.

Resting his boot on the bottom fence rung, Aaron waited for the next competitor to come out of the chute. He'd arrived at the rodeo several hours earlier. In that time, he'd watched half the bull-riding event, all of the calf-roping event, met up with a number of old friends and spent forty-five minutes in the KRDS booth doing a live broadcast with Quick Draw McGraw. He was scheduled for a second broadcast thirty minutes from now and a final one later in the afternoon.

The morning after the opening-day celebration, an assistant producer from the station contacted Aaron. He'd wondered if Quick Draw was all talk and no action when they discussed the rodeo over dinner the previous night. But as his name implied, Quick Draw wasted no time.

In return for the favor, Aaron asked permission to promote the Hailey Reyes Foundation during the broadcasts and to have brochures on the foundation's equestrian-safety program on hand to pass out. The assistant producer was very accommodating and eager to help Aaron with his cause.

"'Scuse me, mister." A small hand tugged on his shirtsleeve. "Can I have your autograph?" A kid no more than seven or eight held out a program and a pen.

"Sure." Aaron had heard this same request a dozen times already today. Two years ago, during the height of his rodeo career, he'd have signed a hundred autographs, a few of them on T-shirts, baseball caps, bald heads and bare bellies.

"What's your name, buddy?"

"Brandon."

The kid wasn't old enough to remember Aaron in his

heyday. More likely, his parents, who were standing over to the side, wanted the autograph but were too embarrassed to ask.

"Here you go, Brandon." Aaron returned the signed program and pen and then ruffled the kid's already messy hair.

"Thanks!" He bolted off, the program clutched to his chest, then showed it excitedly to his parents.

Aaron smiled and tipped his hat at them before turning back to watch the saddle bronc riding.

This and bareback bronc riding had been *his* events, the ones that made him a national champion as well as a celebrity, at least in the world of rodeo. It had also made him plenty of money. Not from competing. Only the best of the best earned enough to live on, and even then not in the lap of luxury.

Aaron received the bulk of his generous income from product endorsements and hosting the cable rodeo show. He took home more money from a single ad in *Western Horseman* magazine than he had his first year on the professional circuit.

Along with rodeoing, he gave up the public limelight when Hailey died. Half of his money still sat in a bank account, collecting interest. He didn't need it, not for the simple lifestyle he preferred. Hailey had been like him in that respect. She was just as content living in his motor home as in the five-bedroom, four-bathroom house he bought her for a wedding present.

He never set foot in the house or motor home again after her accident. Taking his accountant's advice, he sold both last year and used the proceeds to fund the foundation.

Though he didn't know Natalie well, she impressed him as someone who also embraced the simple lifestyle and valued family above all else. Jake may have innumerable personality flaws, but he, too, was a dedicated family man, and Aaron admired and respected him for it.

Jake had clearly pictured someone very different for his sister than a two-bit rodeo bum, as he'd called Aaron, five years younger than her. He accused Aaron of marrying Hailey for her money, having no idea Aaron's annual income was triple what she earned from the trust. Jake still didn't know the true extent of Aaron's finances, and he intended to keep it that way. He would be judged for himself, not his bank-account balance.

Was Natalie someone who put a lot of stock in a person's annual earnings? He doubted it. Thinking of her triggered memories of their kiss last night. He'd taken advantage of her in a weak moment, which was wrong. But everything about their kiss had felt incredibly right, and he'd do it again in a heartbeat.

Explosive applause jarred Aaron from his thoughts and returned him to the present. The saddle bronc riding had come to an end, and the winners' names were being announced over the loudspeaker. Calf roping would start after a fifteen-minute break. Half the people in the stands vacated their seats and piled into the aisles, only to wait in line at the concession stands and restrooms. Aaron figured he should probably grab a bite to eat, too, before returning to the KRDS booth. In a minute or two. After the rush.

"Hey, Aaron! Aaron Reyes. Is that really you?" A tall, lanky man, impeccably dressed in designer western clothes, zigzagged through the crowd toward him. "Well, I'll be dipped in shallow water. It is you."

He was dogged by a sloppily dressed, shaggy-haired camera operator who looked completely out of place at a rodeo. In the two years since Aaron had seen his old cronies, neither had changed one lick.

"Garth. Lonnie." He pushed the brim of his cowboy hat back to get a better look at them. "I should've figured you'd be here."

"How long has it been?" Garth pulled him into a backslapping hug. "And how in the Sam Hill are you?"

"Two years, and I'm doing all right."

"Glad to hear that." He gripped Aaron's shoulder hard before letting him go. "We've missed you, partner. Kenny Jay ain't got near your talent or good looks."

"It's good to see you, too." Aaron reached over and patted

the side of Lonnie's face. "I see you're still hanging around this loser. What? No better offer from one of the big networks?"

Lonnie grinned sheepishly and moved the camera from one arm to the other. "Guess I'm gonna be stuck with him for another year."

"Oh, yeah?"

Garth flashed the winning smile that had helped land him the lead anchor on *Rodeo Week in Review.* "We just got renewed for another season."

"That's great. I'm really happy for you."

"Shoot. I'm doubly happy." Garth's impossibly wide smile actually managed to increase in size. "Kenny Jay won't be coming back. The producers think a new coanchor is in order, and I tend to agree." He made a face and pointed his thumb toward the ground.

"Really?" Aaron watched the show every now and again. He wasn't particularly impressed with his replacement, but neither did he think him completely inept. "So, I take it Kenny Jay's not here?"

"Naw. I'm flying solo for a couple of shows. Until we find a replacement." His eyebrows bobbed so high they disappeared beneath the brim of his very fine, very expensive Stetson. "You aren't by chance looking for a job?"

Lonnie's perpetually hangdog face lit up. "Hey, that's a great idea. Why don't you come back? We could really use you."

Spectators returning to their seats filed past in a noisy stream, many watching them with unguarded interest. More than once, Aaron heard his name and Garth's mentioned. For a moment, he was thrown back in time. Aaron had competed at this same rodeo for seven straight years. The last two years of his career, he'd sat in front of the camera beside Garth, providing color commentary when he wasn't participating in an event.

"I'm not in the market for a job right now." The words were harder to say than he expected them to be.

"What are you doing that keeps you so busy?" Garth asked, his expression curious.

He'd been a real friend to Aaron during the years they worked together and especially after Hailey's death. It was Aaron who'd lost touch with Garth, not the other way around.

"I'm a wrangler at Bear Creek Ranch."

"The resort that belongs to your late wife's family?" Garth and Lonnie exchanged glances.

"Yeah." Aaron could understand their reaction. Both had heard him complain endlessly about the Tuckers and their treatment of him.

Lonnie found his voice first. "Well, that's cool, I guess."

"It's only temporary. In order for me to continue receiving the income from Hailey's share of the family trust, I have to spend eight weeks every year on the ranch."

"Ah. I see."

Aaron didn't much like the tone in Garth's voice. "I'm not doing it for the money. Well, I am, but not for myself. The income from the trust funds the foundation I established in Hailey's name."

"What kind of foundation?" Garth listened intently while Aaron explained.

"That's the reason I'm here today. KRDS invited me to do a live broadcast from their booth. In exchange, I get to promote the foundation and the programs we offer."

Garth's lead-anchor smile emerged in full force. "That's a damn fine thing you're doing. For the kids, and for Hailey. She'd be right pleased."

"I hope so."

"What do you say?" Garth nodded at Lonnie's camera. "Got enough film in that contraption for an interview with Aaron?"

"You bet." Lonnie checked the controls on the camera then hoisted it onto his shoulder. "Light's better on the east side of the arena."

"Let's get a move on." Garth slung an arm around Aaron's shoulders and dragged him along.

"You don't have to do this. But I really appreciate it."

"Why wouldn't we? It's for a good cause. And I'm sure the producers will jump all over the chance to help."

"Thanks." Aaron was suddenly very sorry he'd let two such good friends slip away. He promised himself after today he'd stay in touch.

"Besides," Garth said as they walked, "we ain't about to let some crackerjack local radio station get an exclusive with Aaron Reyes now that you've decided to come out of retirement."

Aaron laughed. His former coanchor always did get excited and jump to conclusions. "I'm not coming out of retirement."

Garth elbowed Aaron jokingly in the ribs. "You sure about that?"

He started to disagree then shut his mouth. The truth was, it did seem a little like he'd come out of retirement. And the feeling fit like a pair of custom-made boots.

"THAT'S A BEAUTIFUL horse you're riding." The woman was referring to Dollar. Her attention, however, was riveted on Aaron. Mostly on his face. Once or twice her gaze wandered to the rest of him, particularly the lower half.

"Thanks."

"Is he yours or does he belong to the ranch?"

"He's mine." For the moment, they were riding side by side. In the places where the trail narrowed, he would drop into line behind her. With any luck, another such spot would appear soon.

"Have you owned him long?"

Her enraptured expression was beginning to make him uncomfortable. "Ten years."

"What color do you call that?"

"Bay." Aaron purposefully kept his answers short so as not to encourage her attempts at flirtation, and his manner friendly so as not to offend or anger her. She was an attractive woman and obviously conscientious about her appearance. Also, a better rider than she let on. Lack of confidence maybe. More likely she wanted an excuse to stick close to the wranglers.

A week in the company of paying guests, and Aaron had already started lumping them into categories. When he mentioned this to his bunkmates, Randy just laughed and congratulated him on becoming a true member of the hospitality industry.

"Have you worked here long?" the woman asked.

"About a month."

"Is that all?" She lifted her sunglasses off her face to give Aaron a peek at her eyes. They were a nice shade of blue. Not nearly as vivid as Natalie's.

Aaron must have inadvertently pulled back on the reins, because Dollar came to an abrupt halt. He gave the horse a nudge. "Walk on, boy."

Dollar shook his head as if confused.

He wasn't the only one. There had been a time when Aaron compared every woman he encountered to Hailey. How soon after he arrived at Bear Creek Ranch had that changed? When he met Natalie? Hugged her at the awards ceremony? Kissed her later that same night?

"Hey. Did you nod off on me?" The woman's jest bordered on accusing.

"Sorry." He touched the brim of his hat. "If you'll excuse me. One of the other riders has a saddle slipping."

He trotted alongside the string of ranch horses and caught up with a guest he picked at random from the group. He instructed the guy on how to shift his weight and straighten a saddle that really wasn't slipping. All so he could escape the attention of a woman whose blue eyes didn't captivate him like Natalie's did.

"Thanks, pal," the guy said, happy to be out of a danger he was never in to begin with.

The day was especially gorgeous and warm for mid-March. It had also been a long day for Aaron. This trail ride was his third in a row. He'd gotten up early, too, after arriving home late from the rodeo.

No, not the rodeo. A country-western bar. Garth, Lonnie and a whole bunch of his old friends talked him into going with them to the Ponderosa Palace. Not since before he met Hailey had Aaron done anything like that. His lack of energy this morning let him know just how out of practice he was at kicking back and stirring it up with his buddies.

The trail ride progressed smoothly for about another ten minutes. They passed the halfway point, and Aaron was looking forward to the remaining half hour being equally uneventful. With the exception of the woman who'd tried to engage him in *un*titillating conversation, all the riders were relatively inexperienced. The horses, on the other hand, were a dependable lot and could be trusted to get their charges home safely.

"Aaron! Take a gander at that." His fellow wrangler, Little Jose, a nineteen-year-old college dropout with a surplus of charm and almost no ambition, hollered from his place at the head of the string. "There on the ridge."

Aaron squinted in the direction Little Jose pointed. Three small, dark-headed figures were picking their way slowly down the slope. Lost guests? They appeared awfully young to be hiking alone in the mountains.

"Hold up, everyone." Little Jose raised his hand in the air. All the riders obediently stopped. "You wanna ride up after them or should I?" he shouted to Aaron.

It was never a question of *should* they go but *who* would go. Though the trail was worn and clearly marked, night fell quickly this time of year. It was easy to lose one's bearings. And these three didn't appear to have so much as a water bottle with them, much less a warm blanket.

"I'll go," Aaron said. "You stay here with the guests."

He spurred Dollar into a lope. Excited after doing nothing but walking sedately for the better part of a week, the horse climbed the rugged and steep slope as if it were a backyard dirt pile.

The children—Aaron was soon close enough to see that

much about them—stopped and waited, almost as if they were expecting him. They certainly weren't frightened by a big horse and strange man riding full speed toward them.

But then, Aaron was no stranger, he quickly realized. These three girls knew him. Were he on better terms with their father, they might have called him uncle.

Aaron pulled Dollar to a stop a few feet below where Briana stood holding the hands of her two younger sisters. They stared unwaveringly at him, their small faces difficult to read.

"Afternoon." His friendly greeting was met with silence. He tried again. "You kids lost?"

"No," Briana said stiffly. "We know where the ranch is." As if to prove it, she inclined her head to the right. "Over there."

"Two miles over there," Aaron said.

"We can make it."

"Mind telling me what you're doing out here?"

"We were hiking with Mommy and Tr—"

"We were bird-watching," Briana said, cutting off her sister. "On a nature walk. For…school. Right?" Her glance flitted from one girl to the other, challenging them to disagree.

"Ow! You're hurting me." The middle girl tried to pry her fingers loose from Briana's killer grip.

"Kind of a rough trail to take for a nature walk." Aaron observed the mussed and tangled condition of their hair, the rips in their shirts and the scratches on their cheeks and arms.

"We've hiked worse trails than this one." Briana stuck her chin into the air.

Aaron almost laughed. The young teen was the spitting image of her father. A Tucker through and through. She and her sisters were obviously exhausted and ready to go home, but she refused to admit it. Not to him, anyway. The two younger girls, heartbreakers in the making, gazed at him with large, pleading eyes that would melt titanium.

"How 'bout it?" Aaron asked. "You want to ride home with us?"

"No, thanks." Briana spoke for the group.

"Your dad'll have my hide if I don't bring you back safely." No matter their differences, Aaron wouldn't leave Jake's daughters to fend for themselves.

"Please, sis. Can't we ride with them?" the middle one asked. "My legs hurt, and I'm thirsty."

"Yeah, we wanna ride home," the youngest one chimed in. Dried streaks on her face showed she'd been crying.

Aaron wondered what had happened with their mother and her boyfriend. The hiking trails were over on the opposite side of the ridge, separate from the horse trails. Not close, but not so far away the girls couldn't walk it.

"Where are your parents?"

"Mommy's with Travis," the youngest one blurted before Briana could stop her. "Daddy's at work."

Travis. The mother's boyfriend. The reason, according to Natalie, that Jake was in a perpetual bad mood. Evidently, so were his daughters. If they ran away from an afternoon hike, they must really dislike him.

"Come on."

Aaron dismounted and reached for the nearest girl, which happened to be the middle one. She came to him with no hesitation and clung to his neck with her thin arms while he boosted her into the saddle. He experienced a brief moment of nostalgia. Back when he was in high school, before he left home to rodeo full-time, he'd given his nieces and nephews rides all the time.

Next, he picked up the youngest girl. She was five, possibly six years old. The feeling of nostalgia grew stronger when she hugged him briefly, yet fiercely. He plopped her onto Dollar's back behind her sister and gave the horse's rump a pat.

Dollar didn't need settling as much as Aaron needed a moment for himself. Jake was a lucky man to have such beautiful, sweet daughters, and Aaron suffered a small but sharp pang of jealousy. Had things gone differently, had the photographer chosen a different moment to take his picture, Aaron and Hailey might have been blessed with a daughter like one of these.

Natalie was right. He should be more tolerant of his ex-brother-in-law. If Aaron had been forced to move away from his children, he'd be in a perpetually bad mood, too.

"Thanks Mr....ah..."

"You can call me Aaron." He placed the middle girl's hands over the saddle horn. "Hold on to this."

"Thanks, Aaron." She smiled shyly.

The youngest one needed no cuing. She wrapped her arms around big sister's waist and held on tight.

"We'll get you a horse to ride when we reach the bottom," he told Briana.

"That's okay. I can walk." She appeared resigned to returning with him.

"You say that now, but I'm betting you'll change your mind about the time we hit the first creek." They started down the slope, Aaron leading Dollar, who slowed his pace to accommodate his young passengers.

"You don't have to be all nice to us just because you were once married to my aunt."

"I'm being nice to you because I happen to like you."

He did, too. Briana had inherited her father's prickliness, but she adored Natalie's baby and took excellent care of her. Also her sisters. Aaron harbored no doubts she'd have gotten the three of them home safely somehow, someway, even if she'd had to carry her sisters, one under each arm.

At the bottom of the hill, Briana took a look at the long, rocky trail looming ahead and promptly accepted Aaron's offer of a ride. After obtaining permission, Aaron put one small child on with his parent and gave the extra horse to Briana. He continued to walk beside Dollar, leading the sisters. Briana didn't thank him exactly, she was infused with too many Tucker stubborn genes for that. But she did glance his way off and on. The moment they hit the stables, Aaron went to the office and called Natalie at the main lodge to report they'd found the girls.

"Thank goodness." He heard her huge sigh of relief over the

line. "Jake only learned a short while ago that they ran off, and he's a wreck."

"Did their mother and her boyfriend make it home yet?"

"Yeah. Everyone's down at the garage, getting ATVs ready to go scouting for the girls. I'll call and let them know you're at the stables."

She hung up without saying goodbye. While Aaron understood the pressing need to contact Jake, he wished they could have talked longer. Giving them each some space after their kiss the other night had seemed like a good idea, but he missed her and wanted to see her again. Not just in passing at mealtimes, either.

Natalie's father and Little Jose helped the guests dismount, asking them about the ride. By the time Aaron walked out of the office, the guests were pacing in front of the hitching rails, walking off the stiffness in their legs.

Aaron went over to the girls, who sat atop, slouched against or hanging on to, the piped railing by the barn. In his hands were three cans of soda he'd swiped from the office refrigerator. "Here you go."

Flavored and sweetened carbonated water helped break down the remaining barriers between them.

"Thanks!" all three said in unison.

"Your folks are on their way."

That remark earned him a trio of frowns, one contemplative, one sad and one decidedly stubborn.

"Mommy and Daddy are gonna be mad as us," the middle girl said around a swallow of soda.

"Probably," Aaron agreed. "But only because they were scared sick about you."

"Way to rub it in." Briana fired invisible daggers at him.

"Hey. I'm just giving you some advice on how to handle this. You apologize to your parents for worrying them, and I bet you a barrel-riding lesson they won't be half so mad at you."

"What makes you think I'd want a barrel-riding lesson?" she demanded with typical fourteen-year-old attitude.

"I've watched you riding in the arena. You're good. You could be better with a few lessons."

She didn't answer, but her demeanor softened—only to harden again a minute later at the sight of her father's truck shooting down the road. She slumped deeper against the railing. Aaron thought he heard her swear under her breath and chuckled to himself. Hailey had possessed the same stubborn streak.

It was then he realized something amazing. He'd thought of his late wife, remembered her, and there had been no pain. No mind-numbing grief. Only pleasure. He actually smiled at Jake when he and the girls' mother came charging at them from the truck.

"Other than a few scratches, they're fine," he said.

Jake spared Aaron the briefest of nods before going straight to his daughters. Everyone hugged and for a moment, the family wasn't divided. It helped that the boyfriend hadn't come along. Aaron, who'd stepped back to give them some room, glimpsed the life his former brother-in-law had once had and, according to Natalie, had fought to keep.

As soon as the parents were assured their children were unharmed, the reprimands started.

"What in heaven's name were you thinking? Taking off like that in the middle of nowhere?"

"Do you have any idea how worried your mother and I were?"

"You could've been hurt. Or one of your sisters."

It didn't stop there.

The youngest girl burst into tears. The middle one looked bleak and hung her head. Briana was made of slightly stronger stuff than her sisters. She stoically faced the music, chewing her upper lip and fiddling with the buttons on her jacket.

During a pause in her father's lecture, she swallowed, shot Aaron a sideways glance and said, "I'm sorry to have upset you and Mom. It was my fault. I'm the oldest and should have known better."

Both her parents recovered slowly.

"Yes, it is your fault." Jake's voice lost some of its angry edge. "But I'm glad to see you taking responsibility."

Briana nodded and went back to chewing her lip.

"Why don't we discuss this at home," her mother suggested in a voice that was no longer one decibel below shrieking.

"Good idea." Jake gathered his daughters in a group and, along with their mother, herded them toward his truck. He abruptly stopped. "Go on. I'll be right there." He turned and came back to Aaron. "Natalie tells me you're the one who found the girls and brought them home."

"It wasn't exactly a rescue operation. They were coming down the mountain by Windy Pass. We just gave them a ride."

"If I know Briana, she didn't want a ride."

"It did require a little arm-twisting."

An odd look crossed Jake's face. When he finally spoke, Aaron understood why. Jake didn't do humility well.

"Thank you for what you did."

"Hey. I enjoyed it. Your daughters are great. You must be proud of them."

"When they're not knee-deep in trouble, they're darn near perfect." Jake hesitated and appeared to think carefully before speaking. "I didn't know you liked kids."

"Yeah. I do." For reasons he couldn't explain, he said, "Hailey and I couldn't decide on how many we wanted, just that we did. And right away."

"Really?"

"You act surprised."

"I am. About you. Not Hailey. Frankly, I didn't figure you for the fatherly type."

"I only wish I'd had the chance. But then…things didn't work out."

"You were planning on starting a family?"

"We already had." Aaron then told Jake something he'd previously kept to himself and thought he always would. "She was seven weeks pregnant when she died."

Chapter Ten

"Breaking ranch rules, Jake? That's not like you."

He'd recognized his cousin Carolina's car when she pulled up in front of Founders Cabin and had all of ten seconds to prepare before she discovered him sitting in the front-porch swing, nursing a beer.

"It's dark outside," he grumbled, not liking the barely concealed amusement he detected in her voice. "And I parked around back."

He'd also left all the interior lights off except for a pewter wall sconce mounted just inside the door. Without the aid of night goggles, a person wouldn't know he was here or see that he was drinking. Carolina must have made an educated guess about where to find him *and* his beverage of choice.

But then, this wasn't the first time he'd spent the night in his grandparents' old home since his divorce, sleeping on the couch in the now conference, former living room. There were days he just couldn't bring himself to leave the ranch, couldn't drive the dark road to that empty house he'd built for himself and his three daughters who were there only every other weekend.

Uninvited, Carolina sat in the chair adjacent to the swing. "I hear the girls are fine," she said after settling in. "That's good."

"Yeah. Very good."

He laid his head back and squeezed his eyes shut, reliving again that awful half hour when he hadn't known their whereabouts or if they were all right. He couldn't remember ever being so scared. Or so relieved when Natalie called him to report that Aaron had returned from a trail ride with his daughters in tow.

Aaron!

The last person he'd have imagined helping him or his children. The one who just told him his sister had been pregnant when she died.

"Did you find out why they took off?" Carolina asked. She dragged an old wooden footstool over and propped her feet up, crossing them at the ankles. Apparently, she intended to stay and pester him a while longer.

"They got mad at Ellen's boyfriend." Though he'd been told the man's name, Jake refused to speak it. "Briana said he was ordering them around and that Ellen let him, telling the girls to listen. They got fed up and ran off when Ellen and he weren't looking." Making out probably, thought Jake bitterly. "Not particularly smart, but can you blame them?"

"Do you think that's what really happened?"

"Why wouldn't I?" He didn't like what his cousin was insinuating.

"Come on, Jake. They're your daughters. They love you to pieces. And you've only been divorced a year. Ellen could bring Santa Claus home and they wouldn't like him."

Bring home?

A sour taste filled the back of Jake's throat. It was *his* home Ellen was bringing men to. The one he'd lived in his entire life and where he thought *he'd* be raising his daughters.

Ellen had met her lover at his home, too, when the girls were at school and Jake was in Payson on business. If not for a canceled appointment, he might never have discovered her affair. Singular. She'd sworn there'd been only one man and only one instance.

Jake didn't believe her.

When the day finally came he moved back into his house, he'd burn every stick of furniture and buy new.

"Whether or not the girls like Ellen's boyfriend isn't my problem," he said, "and I'm sure as hell not going to try to fix it." He took a swallow of his beer but the sour taste in his throat remained.

"Care to tell me what's really got you in a snit?"

"My kids went missing, and my ex-wife is strutting around the ranch with her latest boy toy. I'm thinking that's enough."

"It was nice of Aaron to bring the girls home."

"Real nice."

"Why do you say it all snarly-like? He's not such a bad guy. The guests rave about him."

Guests. What did they know?

"Oh, I get it." Carolina slapped her leg. "You can't stand being grateful to him."

She knew him too well. He needed to spend more time in the company of strangers.

"Fine," Jake growled. "He helped out the girls so they didn't have to walk. Doesn't make him less of a jerk."

"I think it does."

He dropped his head and rubbed his temple. "It's getting late. I'm tired."

Carolina didn't take the hint. "Natalie's pretty into him. She's a good judge of character."

"Except for her kid's father."

"Even she admits his leaving was partially her fault."

"I don't want to talk about Natalie."

"You're not still thinking of changing company policy and forcing her to stop seeing Aaron?"

"They're dating?" Jake sat up straight.

"No. Bad choice of words. But they would be dating if not for you. Right now they're just walking around, ogling each other with their tongues hanging out."

"I could do without the visual."

This time, Carolina did laugh. Loudly.

"I'm going to have to ask you to leave," he said blandly.

"Don't be such a snot." She'd called him that often when she was growing up.

"I've had a bad day. You're not helping."

"You've had a great day, Jake. Your kids are fine. It could have turned out a whole lot worse."

"Did you know Hailey and Aaron were planning on starting a family?" he abruptly asked.

Carolina shifted and recrossed her legs. "Were they?"

"According to Aaron."

"That's not such a shock. Most young married couples contemplate having a family."

Jake swirled the last of his beer around in the bottom of the can. He'd lost interest in finishing it. "They weren't just contemplating. Hailey was pregnant when she died."

"Wow." Carolina didn't speak for a moment. When she next did, her voice was unsteady. "I didn't know."

"Me neither. Until today. Aaron told me."

"That just makes everything so much worse." She sniffed quietly. "Poor Aaron."

"Poor Aaron!" Jake came out of his seat and went to stand by the railing, his movements jerky. "Don't tell me you're feeling sorry for him."

"Of course I feel sorry for him. He lost his wife and his child. That must have been horrible for him."

"He's not the only one who suffered. We all did."

"Hailey was his wife."

"She was my sister. He only met her eight months before the accident."

"I'm not sure loss is something that can be measured by length of acquaintance." She rose from her seat and laid a hand on his shoulder. "He loved Hailey."

"If he loved her so much, then why is he sniffing around Natalie?"

"People aren't made of stone. They recover eventually. Move on. You will, too, someday, though you may not think it now."

She was right about that. He didn't think he'd ever recover from his ex-wife's infidelity. "I wish Aaron would move on somewhere else besides Bear Creek Ranch."

"I think he and Natalie are a cute couple. He could be good for her. God knows, she deserves a decent guy. And he likes kids. Single guys don't exactly flock to women with babies."

"Good for her?" Jake turned away from the railing and in so doing, shook Carolina's hand loose. "You're crazy."

She took his outburst in stride. Unlike him, his cousin maintained her cool under stress. "If they fall in love," she said gently, "and he takes her away from here, there's nothing we can do about it. Or should. It's her life. Her decision. Just like it was Hailey's decision."

"She wouldn't have left home if not for him. Wouldn't have died." Two years had passed since he lost his little sister, and his pain hadn't diminished.

"Hailey didn't leave you, Jake. She went *with* Aaron. There's a big difference, and you have to stop thinking you were abandoned. Or that he caused her death."

"He should have told me she was pregnant."

She should have told him. Hailey wanted children and complained often that, at thirty-three, her biological clock was ticking. That was in part why Jake had been opposed to her quickie elopement to a younger man. In his opinion, Aaron married Hailey for her money and in exchange, she got herself a sperm donor.

"Did it occur to you he might not have told you in order to spare you more hurt?"

"Why?" Jake scoffed. "He can't stand me."

"For the same reason you're still beating yourself up all this time later. Guilt."

"I'm not—"

"Please. We both know your last phone conversation with Hailey was an argument over Aaron. The next day, she dies. Don't tell me you aren't feeling guilty as hell."

He didn't tell her. Because she was right.

"I'm sorry to sound like a meanie, Jake, but hating Aaron, treating him poorly, won't bring Hailey back and it certainly won't alleviate your guilt." She reached again for his arm. "Hailey loved you. And wherever she is, I'm sure she's forgiven you. She'd want you to let go and make peace with Aaron."

Jake flipped his beer can over and dumped the contents into the bushes growing alongside the porch. "That's just it. I don't think I can."

"Let go or make peace with Aaron?"

"Both."

"Fine. Have it your way. Can't say I didn't try."

Carolina did something then almost unheard of for her. She left Jake alone to wallow in his misery. And wallow he did, for most of the long, sleepless night.

NATALIE WAS HAVING one of those mornings. The kind where nothing went right.

She'd started out by loading Shiloh in the car and driving to Payson for her appointment with the child-custody attorney. Natalie had decided to let Drew abdicate his rights to their daughter, and with the attorney's help came up with a response to Drew's request that included visitation should Drew and Shiloh both wish it when she was older. Natalie struggled with that one, but agreed with the attorney it was unfair to deny her daughter the right to know Drew.

The meeting was positive and productive, but also emotionally draining. Natalie had left the attorney's office with a lump in the back of her throat.

On the way home, she stopped to visit a woman whose name had been given to her by a friend of a friend as a possible babysitter. Olivia, Briana and the gals at the ranch were doing great with the Shiloh "babysitting chain," as Natalie called it. However, now that the new season was upon them, the chain occasionally broke down.

Just yesterday, one of the kitchen staff had a personal emergency. Natalie was left without anyone to watch Shiloh for two hours in the middle of the day. Alice bailed her out by agreeing to cover the front desk until the next member of the chain was free. Jake showed more understanding than he could, or should, have. Natalie didn't think she'd squeak by a second time. She needed to make permanent, reliable day-care arrangements.

Two things became immediately apparent the instant she stepped inside the woman's house. First, no way was she going to leave her precious baby in a place where screaming pre-schoolers circled a blaring TV. Second, she didn't want to leave Shiloh anywhere. Her daughter belonged at Bear Creek Ranch.

With that in mind, Natalie drove to the nearby college and posted a job for a nanny in the counselors' office. They'd hired students for part-time help at the ranch before. Maybe she'd luck out.

It was after she returned to the ranch that her morning really started to spiral downward. One problem after another arose and for some reason, no one was available to handle them except her. The guests in cabin twenty-three found a scorpion in their shower. The microwave in cabin fourteen shorted out. A raccoon had gotten into the Dumpster behind the laundry during the night and scattered garbage all over the place.

Because Natalie had no choice, she took Shiloh with her, lugging the baby around in her carrier, a diaper bag, which doubled as a purse, slung over her shoulder.

The worst part of the morning occurred when Natalie learned six cancellations had come in, all for the weekend after next. So far this season, they'd been ahead of previous years. Six cancellations was a lot and put them behind. Jake was meeting with the agent from the insurance company, so Natalie would have to wait until they were done to deliver the bad news. As the minutes ticked by, her agitation increased.

She left the main lodge in a hurry when Shiloh suddenly started crying. Natalie couldn't blame her daughter. She felt like indulging in a good cry herself. While she wouldn't trade motherhood for anything, it wasn't always easy to balance work and family.

Escaping next door to the dining hall, she nursed Shiloh in the kitchen and ate a late lunch, wolfing down a sandwich Olivia fixed for her.

"Some day off, hey, *chiquita?*" Olivia asked. She stood behind Natalie, smiling down at the baby. "Your mama's one busy lady."

Shiloh watched Olivia with interest. Natalie had noticed her baby becoming increasingly aware of her surroundings lately. And stronger. She could lift her head and swivel it from side to side. She'd also started rolling. The other day she nearly rolled off the changing table, scaring Natalie.

"I'm afraid the worst isn't over," she said, returning Shiloh to the carrier and buckling her in.

"Where are you going now?" Olivia continued to make cooing noises in an attempt to engage Shiloh.

"The office. We had some cancellations this morning. The Brubakers called off their wedding. I need to tell Jake about it. Millie, too. She's at an estate sale today. Then home, hopefully. If I'm lucky, Shiloh will nap and no other calls will come in. I have a sinkful of dirty dishes, a clothes hamper ready to explode and a stack of bills to pay."

"It's your day off. Why don't you relax and have some fun."

Natalie caught Shiloh's flailing fist and brought it to her lips. "What do you mean? This is fun." She hugged Olivia and left the kitchen through the back door. "I'll see you later."

At the edge of the outdoor dining area where the employees ate their meals, she stopped cold. Shiloh had messed her diaper. In a bad way. Natalie couldn't go see Jake lugging a stinky baby. Telling him about the cancellations would be bad enough.

She looked around and considered her options. The kitchen was no place to change a dirty diaper. Her car was in the parking lot, a ten-minute hike there and back. The restroom in the main lodge? Okay as long as no guests were in the lobby. Her glance fell on the picnic tables. The place was empty. If she hurried, no one would be the wiser.

Pulling a small blanket from the diaper bag, she spread it out on top of the closest table. Next, she removed a clean diaper, wet wipes and powder, lining them up beside the blanket. Shiloh was last.

She wiggled and fussed while Natalie changed the diaper. Minutes later, with Shiloh strapped back in the carrier, Natalie disposed of their trash in the receptacle beside the door. Hopefully, Shiloh would be her usual complacent self while Natalie spoke with Jake.

"You ready, sweetie pie?"

Shiloh gurgled contentedly, her little rosebud mouth puckering and blowing bubbles. She showed no signs of drowsiness, giving Natalie reason to believe she'd have trouble accomplishing her chores later on.

"Hey. I thought you had the day off." Aaron came toward her from around the corner of the building.

Her heart gave a ridiculously girlish leap at the sight of him. She'd thought a lot about their kiss the other night, how easily she gave in to it and how much she enjoyed it. She'd also thought about her mother's warning that he would be gone by the second week of April. It had taken her months to recover from one man leaving. Something told her recovering from Aaron would be a whole lot harder.

"I was supposed to have the day off, but it hasn't worked out that way."

Not wishing to reveal her nervousness, Natalie attempted casual. Inside was another matter. They hadn't seen each other for three days, and every nerve in her body was springing to life with a great big "hello there."

The afternoon was warm enough that a jacket wasn't necessary. Aaron's faded chambray work shirt was worn thin at the elbows and frayed at the collar. One snap was missing. Yet the shirt enhanced rather than detracted from his good looks. He was all cowboy, and Natalie had a real weakness when it came to cowboys.

"What are you doing here?" she asked, still trying for casual.

He held up an empty coffee can. "Your father sent me on a very important mission."

"You'd better hurry. I know how cranky he gets if he doesn't have his afternoon caffeine fix."

"I've got time." He came to stand beside her, slow and easy as if he belonged there. "Hey, *mija*." He set the empty coffee can down beside the carrier, snatched Shiloh's sock-covered foot and tickled it. "Look at you, growing bigger every day."

Mija?

Natalie's chest contracted. She didn't speak much Spanish, but she recognized the term of endearment parents called their children. Why would Aaron use it with Shiloh? She wasn't his daughter. Natalie warned herself not to place too much significance on the slip, which in all probability meant nothing. Like a coach calling one of his players son.

Before she could respond, the most amazing thing happened. Shiloh smiled. A real smile. And it was aimed right at Aaron. Natalie was simultaneously thrown off guard, filled with delight and immensely disappointed.

"Oh my gosh!" she blurted and squeezed in closer to Shiloh. "Did you see that? She smiled."

"She hasn't before?" Aaron didn't appear all that excited.

"Not really. Sometimes she makes these funny little faces that resemble a smile but aren't." Not according to the countless baby-development books and magazines Natalie regularly consumed. She leaned over Shiloh, braced her hands on either side of the carrier and tried to get her daughter's attention. "Hey there, sweetie pie?" she said in a singsong voice.

Shiloh responded with a giant, slobbery, toothless grin. This one for her mother.

Natalie's knees nearly went out from under her. "She smiled at me."

Her own echoing smile stretched wide. She constantly worried that with other people watching her baby, she'd miss major milestones. Granted, Shiloh's first real smile had been at Aaron, but Natalie had seen it and treasured the moment.

He leaned his head down beside hers. She looked at him, expecting to find him staring at Shiloh, and froze. He was staring at *her*. And the fire burning in his dark eyes triggered a response in her that had nothing whatsoever to do with baby milestones.

"You're so beautiful," he said and reached up to touch the side of her face with tender strokes. It reminded Natalie of the day he'd quieted Shiloh's crying with those same tender strokes, those same strong hands.

"Aaron…"

What was intended as a protest came out sounding like a plea. A plea that was answered when his lips brushed hers.

His kiss was featherlight, honey-sweet. Not at all like the night on her cabin steps. Yet, it affected Natalie as much, if not more, and she fell equally hard under the power of its spell. Leaning into him, she increased the pressure of her mouth and was instantly lost to the world.

The employee dining area was no place for a kiss. Anyone could happen upon them without warning. But the day had been an emotional roller-coaster ride with one incredible high and far too many lows. Aaron's mouth was a balm that both soothed and fortified her.

When he abruptly pulled back, she seized the folds of his shirt, desperate to keep him with her. He straightened. So did she and plastered herself against him. His arms went around her, but he didn't seize the moment and kiss her again. Somehow sensing that she needed close contact more than sexual gratification, he guided her cheek to his chest and rested his chin on her head. Over the sound of his beating heart, she heard him whisper something in Spanish.

"What does that mean?" she asked, nestling more snugly in his embrace.

"You taste incredible."

She tried repeating the phrase in Spanish and butchered it. He laughed softly. She winced.

"It sounds better when you say it."

He said something else, only this time she just listened instead of asking for a translation. They remained locked together for another moment, then two. Sooner than Natalie would have liked, the magic passed and common sense returned. His hands lingered briefly on her arms before releasing her.

"I realize I shouldn't have done that but I'm not sorry I did."

Neither was she, though it couldn't happen again. Certainly not in such a public place. She shuddered to imagine what Jake would have done if he caught them.

Releasing a sigh, she said, "We should talk. Before we get in too deep. Which is where we're headed if you haven't noticed."

"I've noticed. And you're right. We should talk."

Natalie had been thinking later today or tomorrow. When Aaron sat down at the table and motioned for her to do the same, she hesitated before sliding into the seat across from him. Shiloh evidently hadn't found the kiss nearly as interesting as those around her, for she'd drifted off to sleep. Natalie gently moved the carrier so that it faced away from the afternoon sun, using the brief reprieve to collect her wildly scattered thoughts.

"We can't get involved," she said firmly.

"If you're worried that I'm still in love with my late wife—"

"Part of you will always love her. That doesn't bother me."

"What does?"

"You're leaving soon."

"A lot can happen before then."

"Yeah, it can." She could fall head over heels for him. Let him into her life. Grow accustomed to seeing him every day. Yield to the desire building inside her and make love with him. Then, he could leave her with a broken heart. "I'm just not so sure it should."

"The last thing I want to do is hurt you, Natalie."

"I believe you. But it's not that simple. We've got a strong attraction going here, which could get out of control very quickly."

"There isn't any 'could' about it," Aaron said.

"All the more reason for us to exercise control." One wildly scattered thought popped out of her mouth before she could stop it. "Are you planning on staying on after your eight weeks are up?"

"I have some business to take care of in Phoenix," he said. "The foundation has its quarterly board meeting scheduled."

Translation: no.

She'd expected an answer along those lines, shouldn't be so disappointed. But she was, and the futility of any romantic relationship with Aaron hit her hard. There were too many complications, too many obstacles blocking their way.

"I'm not sure this is going to work out between us," she said, her voice wavering.

"I'm more than willing to try." He reached across the table and folded her hands inside his. "But I understand if you're not. Your entire life is wrapped up in this ranch. If anything goes wrong, you're the one with the most to lose."

"We did only just meet last month." She checked on Shiloh as an excuse to look momentarily away.

"You need to do what's best for yourself and your child."

It was the nicest, sweetest thing he could say. "You're not making this any easier."

His thumb found the center of her palm and stroked it. "Really? That's not my intention."

He was such a liar.

"I guess we should start avoiding each other."

"We don't have to," she said, completely mesmerized. He truly had the sexiest hands of any man she'd met. "Just avoid...kissing."

"There's one problem with that." The corners of his mouth curved up. "If I get within ten feet of you, I'm going to kiss you. And the next time we might not escape being seen."

Not *try* but *going to*.

Yikes! Maybe she should spend the next three and a half weeks hiding under her bed, just to be on the safe side.

Or, the less cautious and more adventurous side of her argued, put herself in his path at every available opportunity.

"You aren't the only one doing the kissing," she admitted. "I participated, too." Fully and willingly.

Aaron's eyes took on that same smoky glaze from before, catching her off guard.

"I should stop mentioning kissing."

"Only if you want me to stay away." He flashed her a sexy-as-hell grin that dared her to take him up on the dare.

The back door to the kitchen banged open, and Olivia stepped halfway out. "Alice just called down from the office. Jake's done with his meeting."

Natalie all but ripped her hands from Aaron's. Why, she didn't know. Olivia's eagle eyes were legendary, and she rarely missed a trick. The slitting of those eagle eyes said today was no exception.

"I have to go." Natalie scrambled out of the picnic table and grabbed Shiloh's carrier.

Aaron stood and handed her the diaper bag. "Is everything okay?"

"Yes. No." Natalie went back and forth, and decided to tell Aaron about the cancellations. He was one of the owners and entitled to know everything concerning the ranch. "The Brubaker wedding was called off at the last minute. I need to tell Jake."

"That's bad?"

"They'd reserved six cabins, including the honeymoon one."

"Ouch!" He grabbed the empty coffee can. "You want me to come with you? For moral support," he added.

"I'll be okay." Unfortunately, this wasn't the first time she'd had to give Jake bad news.

"I could watch Shiloh while you're in with him."

A guy offering to babysit? Holy cow! How often did that happen?

"Thanks." She cast a glance at Olivia, who had yet to go inside and wouldn't until Natalie left. "There's a portable crib in the storage room near my desk. I'll just put her there. I don't expect to be in with Jake too long." If he was in the same sour mood he'd been in the last few weeks, she'd hightail it out of there her first chance.

"You sure? Jake won't be happy. I can run interference."

"I'm sure." She'd had plenty of practice over the years. Aaron, however, was a rookie when it came to his former brother-in-law. Jake would eat him alive. She adjusted the diaper bag to a more comfortable position. "I'll see you later."

"Wait." He touched her arm.

Natalie stopped, met his inquisitive gaze with trepidation. She didn't want Aaron to say or do anything of a personal nature. Not with Olivia standing guard at the doorway.

"Does the ranch ever sponsor charity events?"

Not what she'd been expecting to hear. "Um…sometimes. In the past. Why do you ask?"

"I just had an idea." His face took on an odd expression.

"What?"

"I'll tell you later. Maybe. I have to work out some details first." He bounded up the steps into the kitchen and disappeared inside. Olivia shut the door behind him.

"That was bizarre," Natalie murmured to herself and cut across the lawn adjoining the dining hall and the main lodge.

Aaron's odd look and cryptic remark stayed with her up until the moment she met with Jake to inform him of the cancellations.

Chapter Eleven

"Good afternoon. Welcome to Trinkets and Treasures. Something tells me you're not in the market for antiques."

Aaron removed his cowboy hat. "No, ma'am. I'm not."

Jake's aunt Millie beamed at him. "Then to what do I owe the pleasure?"

"Business."

"Antique business?"

"Bear Creek Ranch."

"I see."

She motioned for him to follow and led him on a winding path through a store crowded with everything from tiny jeweled music boxes to glittering beveled mirrors to ornately carved armoires. In the far corner of the store, behind a hand-painted screen, sat an old metal desk and beside it a rickety visitor chair. Holdovers from thirty years ago. And in spite of their battered appearance, quite possibly the newest pieces of furniture in the place.

"Coffee?" she asked.

"If you have any."

She pulled a thermos from under the desk and with it, a pair of ceramic mugs. "Deana filled this at the convenience store up the road right before she left for the day," she said, removing the thermos lid and pouring the coffee. "But if I was a gambling woman, which I am, I'd bet you already know she's not here."

"Gary might have mentioned it."

Millie chuckled, low and lusty. "Don't ever trust him with a secret." She passed a steaming mug to him. "There's cream and sugar in the back if you need it."

"Black's fine."

"So, what's this ranch business that's so gosh darn important you drove clear into Payson to talk to me about it?"

Aaron extracted a folded sheet of paper from his shirt pocket. He was no stranger when it came to presenting business plans. In establishing the Hailey Reyes Foundation, he'd dealt with a whole slew of accountants, bankers, administrators and government agents. Facing Jake should be a cakewalk.

It would, however, be easier with an ally in his corner. Namely, Millie. But he'd have to win her over first, and she wasn't an easy sell.

"The other day Natalie mentioned we had six cancellations."

"Yeah. The Brubaker wedding party. Such a shame. For us and for the bride. I heard the groom changed his mind at the last minute."

"Better now than after they've been married a while, bought a house and had a couple of kids."

"I guess there's a bright side to everything."

"Possibly for the ranch, too."

She sipped her coffee and peered at him over the rim. "I'm listening."

"I know a man in Colorado who lost his daughter ten years ago to a drug overdose."

"I'm sorry to hear that."

"A couple years later he decided to find some good in his daughter's death. He established an annual trail ride. For a two-hundred-and-fifty-dollar donation, couples go on a four-hour ride that ends with a catered steak dinner. All profits go to the Boulder Center for Teenage Drug Abuse."

"How nice."

"Every year, the ride grows bigger. Last year alone, he raised over twenty thousand dollars for the center. Almost a hundred thousand since he started the ride."

She whistled. "That's a lot of money."

"That's a lot of changed lives."

The bell over the front door tinkled.

"Excuse me." Millie wound her way back through the store, only her head visible above the hundred pieces of furniture crammed into a space designed to hold twenty-five. "May I help you," he heard her call.

At least she hadn't run him out of the store yet. Aaron only half listened to her conversation with the customer, mentally reviewing the points he planned on making. A few minutes later, she returned.

"Some guy trying to sell me an old TV," she said, sitting back down.

"You don't take TVs?"

"I said old. Not vintage. I sent him to the pawnshop three blocks over." She glanced curiously at his notes. "I'm not sure what your story has to do with Bear Creek Ranch. Unless you're wanting your friend to move his ride here."

"No." He turned the paper around so Millie wouldn't have to read it upside down. "I'm suggesting we have our own ride here. One where the profits go to the Hailey Reyes Foundation."

"A lovely thought. But how exactly will this benefit the ranch?"

Here was the moment he'd been rehearsing for all morning. He launched into his pitch.

"We could offer accommodations to the participants at a discounted rate. Corrals for their horses. After a long afternoon ride and a late dinner, some are bound to stay over rather than pack up and drive home. We can also make rental horses available for anyone without their own to ride."

"Also at a discount?"

"Or even at no charge. Expenses come right off the top. I talked to my accountant this morning and she said we can write off most of our indirect expenses, including overhead and administrative."

"What about offering lunch as opposed to dinner? Just to make your ride a little different. Or better yet, breakfast. Participants could spend the night before the ride at the ranch."

"And afterward, too. If we give them a reason to stay."

She smiled. "You have something in mind."

"A silent auction."

"I like it." She slid the paper across the desk toward him. "When are you planning on having this ride? Next year when you come back?"

"Two weeks from tomorrow."

"Before you leave?" she said incredulously. "That doesn't give us much time."

Aaron nodded slowly. "I know."

Recently, he'd been debating staying on a while longer. His obligations weren't so demanding they couldn't be postponed. And then there was Natalie. If ever a man had a reason to remain at Bear Creek Ranch, it was her. Another week or two, he might be able to wear down her resistance.

Did he even want to?

Not if he hurt her.

Millie's enthusiasm, so contagious a minute ago, waned the next. "The cause is a worthy one, and I'd be inclined to support it if only because Hailey would have loved a ride in her honor." She frowned, tilted her head to one side. "But a ride this size is a tremendous amount of work for something that won't net the ranch much income, if any." She wasn't being negative, just asking the kind of questions Jake would.

"You have to look at the long term as well as the short term. Say, we rent those six empty cabins."

"Five. We got a reservation yesterday."

"Five then. At a discounted rate, we only break even. But five cabins at a reduced rate beats five empty cabins. At least we're covering our operating costs."

The bell tinkled again. This time, Millie left for ten minutes to tend the customers who had put an item on layaway and were there to pick it up. Aaron used the time to place a call to his friend and former coanchor, Garth, and got the answer he'd hoped for.

"You really think we can rent those cabins?" Millie asked, returning to her chair.

"I guarantee it. I know a lot of people. Give me until tomorrow morning, and I'll have those cabins booked."

She studied at him with new interest. "Keep talking."

"We solicit donations from local businesses as another way to keep the costs down. Offer them free advertising in return. Printing companies for flyers. Grocery stores for food and paper products. Merchants for the silent-auction items. Put Alice in charge. She has a real knack for convincing people to part with something valuable."

"It would be good promotion for the ranch," Millie said thoughtfully.

"It would be great promotion. I might even be able to pull some strings and get *Rodeo Week in Review* to come out and cover the event. I know they'd give us a mention for sure. And the person who does the foundation's Web site for me has already agreed to build a separate one for the trail ride at no charge."

The phone rang, and Millie took the call. "I don't think we can swing it in two months, much less two weeks," Millie said after finishing with her customer.

"No. But we can swing a scaled-down version. Hailey was well-known around here. People will respond. Spread the word for us. Quick Draw and KRDS have already agreed to donate ten commercial spots during peak listening hours and conduct an on-air interview with me the Wednesday before the ride."

"Hmm," she murmured thoughtfully. "You've been a busy boy."

"There's more."

"I can hardly wait."

"Do we have a list of e-mail contacts for past guests?"

"Of course."

"Have Alice e-mail a newsletter to guests within a reasonable driving distance."

"You surprise me, Aaron. You're quite the businessman." Millie gave him an appreciative once-over. "I had no clue." Her expression turned to one of delight. "I don't think Jake has any clue, either." She sat up and rubbed her hands together. "This should be fun."

"I'm going to meet with him as soon as he'll agree to see me." Aaron relaxed for the first time since he'd set foot in Trinkets and Treasure. "I was hoping you'd go with me."

"Are you joking? I wouldn't miss it. But your plan still has some glitches that need to be worked out first. Let's get together after dinner tonight at my place. Bring all your stuff."

Aaron stood, only to bend down and kiss her on the cheek. "Thanks."

"Save the mushy stuff till after we meet with Jake." She shooed him away and picked up the phone. "Let's call him now and set up a meeting time."

"WHAT ARE YOU majoring in?"

"Finance. Though I'm thinking of changing to global economics."

Intelligent and career-oriented, thought Natalie, jotting a note on the résumé in front of her. Attractive and nicely dressed, too. Perhaps too nicely dressed. Would she stick Natalie with a hefty dry-cleaning bill if Shiloh spit up on that silk blouse?

"That's an ambitious major," Natalie commented.

"I'd like to go into international banking after graduation. Live abroad, if at all possible."

She radiated poise and confidence. What she didn't radiate was even the tiniest hint of maternal tendencies. She was pleasant enough and personable. But nanny material? Natalie had her doubts.

They were using Alice's office for the interview that Natalie had scheduled during her lunch hour. Jake's assistant wasn't there. She'd called in sick after going home early the previous day with fever and a sore throat.

"How many children do you think you'd like to have?" Natalie asked the young woman.

"I'm not ready for a family yet and won't be for a while," she said with such gravity she might have been testifying at a senate hearing. "This summer I'm entering a two-year internship program."

"In Payson?"

"No. Phoenix."

Meaning she'd be leaving in a few months. Probably about the same time Shiloh got attached to her.

"And, of course, it would depend on my husband. Not that I have one." Her smile came off as forced. "I'd like to focus on my career before getting married. Starting a family too early can be a mistake, don't you think?"

It hadn't been for Natalie.

"I suppose that depends." A long explanation, Natalie mused, and the woman hadn't even answered the question.

This wasn't someone she could picture pulling up Shiloh's T-shirt and blowing raspberries on her belly. Which was precisely the quality Natalie wanted in the person who cared for her daughter. More than intelligence, more than poise and ambition and nice clothes.

She'd interviewed a different young woman the previous day and liked her very much. Only one problem. With her current classload, the woman could only work two weekday afternoons and Saturdays.

Natalie decided in that instant to call the first candidate and offer her the job part-time. It would take some pressure off the Shiloh babysitting chain and give Natalie the time she needed to continue looking. Maybe she'd luck out and find another good part-time nanny. Then the two of them could job share.

Now, how to end the interview with Miss International Banking?

"Did you bring any references with you?"

"I did." She handed Natalie a sheet of paper from the portfolio sitting in her lap.

Natalie glanced at the names and phone numbers. All were teachers and business owners. Not one child-care or other baby-sitting reference.

"Thanks. I'll need a day or two to check on these."

The desk phone rang, and Natalie picked up the receiver, grateful for the interruption.

"Hello."

"Where's Alice?" Jake didn't bother with a greeting.

"She called in sick today. Remember?"

He muttered a swearword. "I forgot."

Natalie glanced at the young woman and whispered, "Excuse me."

She was indeed smart. Evidently sensing the interview was over and that she wasn't going to receive a spontaneous offer of employment, the young woman collected her things and stood. "Thank you," she murmured and showed herself out.

"Is there something I can help you with?" Natalie asked Jake.

"Yeah, come in here. And bring Alice's laptop. I need you to take some notes for a meeting I'm having."

"I'm the only one manning the front desk today." Lunchtime was typically the slowest part of the day. Natalie had transferred the phone into Alice's office and activated the lobby door chime so she could hear any guests come in.

Another swearword from Jake. "We'll just have to manage."

"Be right there." Natalie dropped the résumé off at her workstation before going into Jake's office. Whoever he was meeting with must be important. Having a warm body at the front desk was a top priority with him.

She came to a halt upon entering his office and seeing the two people seated in his visitor chairs. Aaron and Millie. What could they be discussing with Jake that required note taking? And why hadn't the rest of the family been called?

Recovering her composure, Natalie went to the couch on the

far wall, took a seat and opened the laptop. Aaron and Millie both looked her way. Millie's eyes sparkled. Aaron's were dead serious.

Since meeting him, Natalie had watched her father's rodeo DVD collection twice and recognized Aaron's expression. It was the same one he wore when he sat astride a bronc, right before the chute opened.

"I'm all set," she said to Jake, opening a blank page and inserting a header. Though no secretary, she'd performed similar duties in the past before Jake hired Alice, who knew what was expected of her.

"Aaron's laid out a preliminary plan," Millie said by way of starting. "And I think he's done a good job of covering the basics."

"Do you have an extra set of these for Natalie?" Jake asked, reading the papers on his desk.

"Yes." Aaron moved to rise but Natalie beat him to the punch by setting aside her laptop and springing off the couch to take the papers from his outstretched hand.

Once again, she was impressed by his clear focus, evident in the eyes that locked briefly with hers. This was a side of him she hadn't seen before. A side that elicited a whole range of responses in her. Admiration. Respect. Appreciation.

Why had she ever thought he couldn't hold his own with Jake?

Returning to the couch, she scanned the cover page. The words she read were heart wrenching, yet uplifting, and affected her profoundly. Her reaction, however, probably didn't begin to compare to that of the other people in the room, all of whom had known Hailey better than Natalie and loved her. Setting the papers down on the cushion beside her, she typed in "The Hailey Reyes Foundation Annual Breakfast Trail Ride."

Aaron took control of the meeting, explaining the plan in detail. Several times Natalie got so involved in listening, she forgot to take notes and had to scramble to catch up.

What a great idea! A win-win situation for everyone. The foundation, the ranch, the contributors and the riders. Not to mention the many children who would have a safer riding experience because of equipment purchased with the money raised. It would be a lot of work over the next twelve days, but could be done if started right away. By next year, if all went well, they could double the size of the event *and* double the money raised.

Here was the reason for Aaron's odd look and cryptic remark yesterday in the employee dining area.

"I don't disagree that the ranch would benefit," Jake said when Aaron finished. "But to what degree? And will the benefit be enough to make such an undertaking worthwhile?"

His bark, Natalie knew, was worse than his bite. Her boss had long ago acquired the ability to separate family from business and would do what was best for the ranch regardless of his personal feelings. Not an easy feat.

"Have either of you contacted Howard?" he asked, referring to the family trust attorney.

"I faxed him a copy of the plan this morning," Aaron said, "and told him we might be calling this afternoon."

He'd used the fax and the printer? Natalie hadn't seen him come into the office, and she'd arrived before seven. Millie must have taken care of it for him. They did seem quite buddy-buddy, Natalie mused. When had that happened?

"Let's see what he has to say." Jake picked up his phone and a minute later had the attorney on the line. He pushed the speaker button so everyone in the office could hear both sides of the conversation. "In a nutshell, what's your opinion of this breakfast trail ride?" he asked Howard after summarizing their discussion so far.

"It's a good idea if executed correctly. As is starting out small," the attorney elaborated. "Should the ride flop, your loss would be minimal."

"You're saying there's a risk the ranch could lose money?"

"There's risk with everything. But keep in mind, a loss is

tax deductible, which makes it a bit more tolerable. In my opinion, however, you're going to come out ahead. How much ahead will depend in large part on you. The plan is well thought out. Aaron did a good job."

Jake's demeanor as he stared at Aaron gave away nothing. Natalie was a different matter. If he was to glance in her direction, he'd find her flashing him the thumbs-up sign. She was happy for him, pleased at the potential positive outcome of the ride and undeniably impressed.

Howard and Jake asked additional questions, which were answered by Aaron and Millie. Natalie took notes along with creating a list of follow-up items. For Aaron's plan to work, organization was crucial. And commitment. She had faith the employees would work overtime if necessary.

"Thanks, Howard," Jake said. "I'll call you later. Let you know what we decide." He disconnected with the attorney.

"Well?" Millie inquired expectantly.

Natalie, too, waited nervously for Jake's response.

"Let's dwell on it for a day or two." He picked up a pencil and started tapping the eraser on his desk.

"We don't have a day or two." The steel in Aaron's voice matched the hard set of his jaw.

"Why not? There's no rush."

"There is if we want Aaron here," Millie said. "Which we do. It's his connections that will enable us to pull this off."

At the reminder of his leaving, Natalie stopped typing. Listening to him talk about the breakfast trail ride, being swept up in the tide of his excitement, it had been easy to forget he'd be gone in another three weeks.

"He can come back." Jake answered matter-of-factly.

Hope surged in Natalie, only to be dashed.

"I can't," Aaron countered. "Not right away."

"Busy?"

"Come on, Jake," Millie admonished. "You, too, Aaron. Let's stay on track, please." She put each man in his place with a stern look. "When Aaron can or can't return to the ranch is irrelevant. We all know April's the perfect month for the ride. The weather's gorgeous. There are no holidays to create a conflict. People aren't leaving on vacation."

"There's a lot to do in a short time." Aaron picked up where Millie left off. "The sooner we get started the better."

"We can have enough of the family here tonight for a quorum," Millie appealed to Jake. "Present the plan and take a vote."

"And if they're against the plan?"

"I'll bribe them."

He shot her a disapproving frown.

"Come on," she teased. "Lighten up."

"What about you?" He turned his attention to Aaron. "How will you feel if the family votes no?"

"I'll abide by whatever they decide. But be warned, I'm going to do my absolute best to convince them to vote yes."

Natalie stared at him in awe. Here sat a man brimming with confidence, burning with drive and consumed with passion for a cause he believed in. Aaron the cowboy was sexy. Aaron the businessman stole her heart. And, to be completely honest, incited a desire within her she hadn't felt in a long time, if ever.

"I'll start placing calls to the family." Millie was the first on her feet. "Seven-thirty okay with everyone?"

"Yes," Jake said. He and Aaron, apparently forgetting Millie's warning, were locked in visual combat over his desk.

Natalie powered down the laptop. She knew she was expected to leave and return to the front desk, not hang around. At the door to Jake's office, she caught the tail end of his remark to Aaron. It stopped her cold.

"This may surprise you, Reyes, but I'm going to do my absolute best to convince the family to vote yes, too."

She reached for the doorjamb with her free hand, needing something solid to hold on to.

If she wasn't mistaken, the earth had just moved.

NATALIE STOOD at Alice's desk, her back to the door, and scrawled a hasty note explaining about the meeting minutes she'd taken and the follow-up list. She then taped the note to the top of the laptop, which she set in the center of Alice's desk. At the click of the office door closing, she spun around, her involuntary retreat halted by the desk pressing into the backs of her thighs.

Aaron came toward her, tall, broad-shouldered, his stride purposeful. Natalie immediately jumped to all kinds of conclusions, every one of them having to do with the closed door and the fact they were alone together.

She watched him advance, her insides in turmoil. He'd shown her a different side to himself today, one she'd found irresistible.

Did he sense her changing feelings toward him and intend to do something about it?

"I thought Alice might want this list of my contacts." He handed Natalie a piece of paper.

"Ah…okay." Talk about misreading signals.

She took the paper, turned sideways and laid it next to the laptop. When she turned back around, Aaron was standing so close, one deep breath and she'd be snuggled up against him.

"D-didn't we agree n-not to do this?" she stammered.

"We agreed not to kiss. I don't remember anything about being in the same room together."

"Same room together? Any nearer and we'd be—" She stopped short, distracted by the sensual currents flowing between them.

They couldn't risk another semipublic indiscretion. Not with Jake in the next office. Natalie ducked and slipped out from between Aaron and the desk. She retreated a safe distance, which wound up being a mere two feet. Alice didn't have a large office.

"That's a really terrific idea you had for the breakfast trail ride," Natalie said. Safe distance, safe subject.

"I'd like to take all the credit, but the fact is, I stole it from a friend in Colorado."

"It's still terrific. There's nothing like it in these parts."

He leaned against the desk where seconds ago she'd been standing, giving her that same slow, I'm-just-a-simple-cowboy smile he had that first day he arrived. Except now she knew better. Aaron was no simple cowboy.

"The family will vote to have the ride," she said confidently. "You have nothing to worry about. Especially with Jake behind you."

Aaron pushed his hat back on his head, his expression changing to one of bafflement. "Never thought I'd live to see the day he'd side with me on anything."

"Jake's a smart businessman. He knows a winning proposition when he hears it. The last couple years have been lean. He not only kept the ranch afloat, he turned a profit. Small, but better than losing money."

"I know. I get the quarterly reports."

"And he did it in the wake of losing his sister."

"You don't have to cheer him on. My problems with him have nothing to do with the ranch or his management of it."

"I may not always agree with him. And, yes, his temperament since his divorce leaves a lot to be desired. But he's a good manager, a good boss and you won't find a better friend."

"Or a more dangerous enemy?"

"Perhaps."

"You're hedging."

"A little."

"I'm not afraid of him, Natalie."

"No, I don't think you are."

Aaron inched closer, narrowing the safety zone she'd created to a thin ribbon. "Say the word, and I'll battle Jake to the bitter end for you and Shiloh."

Her *and* Shiloh. Oh, sweet heaven. He didn't just want her, he wanted her baby, too.

"Please," she whispered. "I need more time." Why did she have to be so sensible? Why couldn't she throw herself at him and to hell with the consequences?

Because she had a daughter to think about. A job. A family.

A home. And not being sensible, not looking before she leaped, was what landed her in trouble before.

"There's no one at the front desk. I have to get back." A cop-out, yes, but a necessary one. Natalie was in no shape emotionally to resist Aaron.

"Okay." He didn't move from Alice's desk, making it clear to both of them she was the one retreating and he was the one willing to take a stand. "I'll see you at the meeting tonight."

"Meeting tonight?"

"Won't you be there to take notes again?"

She'd forgotten about Alice being sick. "Um, I guess." She'd have to check with her mother to see if she could babysit.

"Would you like me to pick you up and drive you to Founders Cabin?" he asked.

"That's not necessary. I have the golf cart."

"Then will you pick me up and drive me there?"

"If you'd like." She worked for him and couldn't refuse. At least, that was the excuse she gave herself.

"I'd like. See you at seven-fifteen."

How could something so innocuous sound so seductive? She really had to get out of Alice's office fast.

"Olivia was right about something she said to me yesterday."

"Oh?" Natalie paused with the door half opened.

"She told me not to play around with you unless I was playing for keeps."

"Sounds like her," Natalie answered weakly.

"I told her not to worry." His voice drifted over her like an intimate caress. "When I play, *querida,* it's always for keeps."

Chapter Twelve

"Thanks for coming. Nice to see you. Glad you made it."

Aaron tipped his cowboy hat, shook hands, smiled and clapped shoulders on his way out of the dining hall. He had exactly three minutes to meet up with Quick Draw for their scheduled broadcast.

The last two weeks had been one big blur, with everyone on the ranch working their collective butts off. The end result, however, was well worth it. Nearly two hundred participants had shown up for the breakfast trail ride, well exceeding everyone's expectations.

As Aaron promised Millie, the five canceled cabins were rented, along with three more. He had high hopes they'd be booked solid before the end of the day. And why not? Mother Nature had cooperated by giving them a beautiful day, rental rates were discounted, the trails lush with foliage and the fishing excellent. Who could resist staying another night?

The dining hall wasn't large enough to accommodate the large crowd. Dozens of people spilled outside in search of a chair, bench, log or anyplace they could sit while eating. Representatives from the local merchants who'd contributed were also present and mingling with the participants. A reporter from the *Payson Gallop* was on the grounds, snapping pictures and conducting interviews.

"Sorry I'm late," Aaron said to Quick Draw, distracted again by another old friend waving at him.

The KRDS DJ sat at a table in the corner of the parking lot nearest the main lodge. Two techies hovered around him, running equipment and keeping spectators from tripping over the many wires running to the colorfully painted van behind him.

"No problem. Hey, there's someone I want you to meet." Quick Draw indicated a woman standing near the table. "Aaron Reyes, this is Kate Drummond from Air Waves Communications, the parent company of KRDS."

"How do you do?" She offered her hand to Aaron.

"Fine. And yourself?"

With so much on his mind, Aaron found it hard to listen while the woman explained about Air Waves and the ten radio stations they owned in four western states, all but KRDS located in major markets. Before Aaron had a chance to ask her what brought her to the ranch, Quick Draw recruited him for his spot in the live broadcast.

"We're here today for the first annual breakfast trail ride," the DJ said into the microphone, "the proceeds of which go to the Hailey Reyes Foundation. With me is my good buddy Aaron Reyes, former national rodeo champion, head of the foundation and one of the owners of Bear Creek Ranch."

"Thanks for having me again, Quick Draw."

"You chatted with us about the foundation and its equestrian-safety program earlier this week," Quick Draw said, referring to Aaron's phone interview the previous Wednesday. "But why don't you tell us again for those listeners just tuning in."

Aaron recapped the mandate of the foundation and the safety program, trying to be energetic and entertaining. Not easy with only four or five hours' sleep most nights this week.

He caught sight of Natalie strolling up the walkway to the main lodge, engaged in an animated conversation with a guest. He promptly tripped up, forgetting what he was about to say.

Quick Draw adeptly covered for him so that no one listening would notice.

Aaron nodded his thanks.

Quick Draw's broad wink implied he didn't blame Aaron for messing up.

Natalie was lovely to watch. She obviously enjoyed her job. It showed in her sunny smile, the comfortable and relaxed manner in which she moved and her skill at making each guest feel special. If she were to leave Bear Creek Ranch, where else could she go and find a job that suited her like this one did? A place where she not only worked but belonged?

Aaron had traveled much of the western United States. Rodeoing had also taken him to parts of Mexico and Canada. In all the cities he visited, he'd discovered only two women who made him think of settling down. Both had grown up on Bear Creek Ranch.

"I understand you have some interesting facts about the number of head injuries every year due to falls from horses," Quick Draw asked, moving the interview along.

"Most people don't put a whole lot of thought into horse-related accidents." Aaron cited the information given to him by the foundation's statistician, then explained how the figures could be dramatically reduced by wearing helmets.

He and Quick Draw exchanged several more questions and answers, with the DJ occasionally interjecting a joke to keep things lively. Not long after, he wrapped up the interview.

"How can our listeners learn more about the foundation?"

"Visit our Web site." Aaron gave the address. "There's all kinds of good information on how an organization or equine youth program can apply for assistance in purchasing helmets."

"And to make a donation?"

"You bet. The address and phone number are both there."

"Thanks again, Aaron. It's always a pleasure talking with you."

"Always a pleasure being on your show."

"Tell me, what's in store for you next? I understand you're leaving Bear Creek Ranch soon."

"I, ah, have some business back in Phoenix." Aaron's glance went straight to Natalie. She'd finished her conversation with the guest and was standing on a small rise, watching him. They were separated by a good thirty feet. The distance did nothing to diminish the connection he felt with her. "After that, I'm not sure. I've really enjoyed working here."

He meant every word. Since coming to Bear Creek Ranch, parts of him he thought shriveled and dead had come back to life.

"Will you be returning next year?"

"Absolutely."

For the past two weeks he'd managed not to be alone with Natalie only because they both had been so busy getting ready for the breakfast trail ride. During the day, he'd had little time to think about her and the many possibilities his mind conjured. Nights, however, were a different story. She was as much responsible for his lack of sleep as was his overloaded schedule.

He'd left the decision in her hands. She'd apparently chosen the ranch and her job over a relationship with him. He didn't blame her. She not only had a great job but a wonderful environment in which to raise her daughter, one close to her parents. He didn't even have a real home anymore. Supposing Natalie did consent to leave with him. He couldn't take her and Shiloh to the small handyman quarters on his friend's dairy farm outside Laveen where he stayed when he wasn't traveling.

Not that he'd consider asking Natalie to leave with him at this point. He'd lived at Bear Creek Ranch for seven weeks, kissed her twice, yet they were still relative strangers. They needed to know each other better before making any serious decisions.

He had nine days left. Longer if he postponed the quarterly board meeting.

The more he thought about it, the more the idea of staying on appealed to him. He'd call his banker, accountant and attorney tomorrow and move up the board meeting to the last week of April. After the meeting and a long-overdue visit to his mother, he'd return to Bear Creek Ranch.

"Well, good luck to you, Aaron," Quick Draw said, bringing the interview to a close.

"Thanks." He shook the DJ's hand. "I'll see you around."

"Maybe sooner than you think."

Funny, that was supposed to be Aaron's line.

NATALIE HAD DISAPPEARED inside the main lodge sometime near the end of Aaron's interview. He made his way there now. Breakfast was still going, and the ride wasn't scheduled to start for another half hour. If she wasn't too busy, he'd take her aside and speak to her. He didn't quite know what he'd say but he had a whole ninety seconds before he hit the lobby door to think of something.

He wiped his damp brow. Not since he'd asked Ann Marie Chavez to the homecoming dance in eleventh grade was he this nervous about approaching a woman.

Long tables had been set up on the porch and inside the lobby, displaying the silent-auction items. People bunched in front of the tables, inspecting the auction items and writing down their bids. Aaron was forced to wait at the top of the steps for the crowd to thin enough that he could squeeze through. He glanced at some of the bid sheets on his way to the door. The amounts were encouraging. Late last night, he'd run some preliminary numbers based on the monies received to date. That amount would go up considerably after the silent-auction proceeds were added in.

Not bad for two weeks. Imagine what they could do next spring with a whole year to plan and prepare.

Aaron came to a sudden halt.

When had he started including himself with the rest of the Tuckers?

Strange, but it felt right.

"Mr. Reyes? Do you have a moment?" The woman he'd met earlier from Air Waves Communications brushed up beside him.

"Just one. I'm meeting someone inside." He was usually good at names. Hers escaped him.

She saved him the trouble by handing him her business card. "Would it be possible to make an appointment with you tomorrow or the day after?"

"Regarding what—" he glanced at her card "—Ms. Drummond?"

"A job."

"You looking?"

She smiled. "I'm offering."

"Me?"

"I think you could be just what Air Waves is in the market for."

"And what's that?"

Guests jostled them from all sides, bumping and shoving.

"Why don't we go over there." She motioned to the far end of the porch where there were less people.

He'd told her he could only spare a minute yet he found himself giving her more.

"I didn't come to Bear Creek Ranch just to watch the KRDS live broadcast, Mr. Reyes."

"Call me Aaron. And why are you here?"

"To observe you in person. See if my hunch is correct." Jeans and an embroidered cowboy shirt didn't diminish her very polished appearance. Ms. Drummond could conduct business wearing a potato sack and still come off like a female version of Donald Trump, only nicer. "You caught our interest during the Payson Rodeo. Since then, I've watched a lot of old *Rodeo Week in Review* episodes."

"Excuse me for saying this, Ms. Drummond, but you need to get a life."

Her laugh was bright and very controlled. "You were good. Charming and charismatic. Sometimes qualities that work well in television don't lend themself to radio. Not so in your case. The station was inundated with calls and e-mails after your broadcast at the rodeo with Quick Draw. Ratings soared again this week on the morning of your phone interview. Our audience likes you and, it appears, will tune in to listen to you."

"If you're not careful, I'm going to get a swelled head."

"You have a talent, Aaron," she said with utmost seriousness. "Nothing wrong with knowing your abilities. Or making use of them."

"I was joking."

"I'm not. We have a need, and I believe you're the right person to fill it."

"What need is that?" he asked, intrigued in spite of his determination to remain disinterested.

"The radio stations owned by Air Waves periodically share prerecorded broadcasts. It's a practice that's proven to be successful and one we'd like to expand. Possibly even offer the broadcasts outside of Air Waves."

"Syndication?"

"Of a sort. I can explain the details in our meeting," she added.

"Where do I fit in?"

Her smile brightened considerably. "The talent, of course."

"What kind of show?"

"We have a few ideas but would like your input before we finalize the concept."

Including him on the decision, making it harder for him to refuse. Smart thinking on their part.

"Let me know what day works best for you, and I'll have the producer fly out from Denver to meet you. He's a big fan." She mixed a fair amount of flattery with a generous portion of insistence.

His friend Garth's remark about Aaron coming out of retirement came back to haunt him.

"How much travel would be involved?" he asked.

"Two to four days every week, depending on the location." She raised a finely penciled brow. "Is that a problem?"

"Ma'am, I've done nothing but travel two to four days a week since I turned eighteen." Except, he realized, these last seven weeks he'd spent at the ranch. He briefly wondered why he didn't miss a way of life that had been ingrained in him for over a decade.

Could it be this place? Natalie?

His requisite annual stint on the ranch was up in another week. Making a permanent home here wasn't something he could do. Not unless the Tuckers agreed to it, and Aaron didn't see that happening.

He shook his head to clear it and said to Ms. Drummond, "I'm sorry. I missed that last part."

"We want you on board, Aaron, and we're prepared to sweeten the pot."

People continued to parade in and out of the lobby door in a steady stream, with more parading out. Aaron glanced at his watch. The ride was starting in fifteen minutes. Most of the horses were already saddled and waiting, either tied up to their owners' horse trailers or down at the stables. He had a lot still to take care of but had yet to talk to Natalie. Neither had he thought of what to say to her.

"I'm sorry to have to cut this short, Ms. Drummond. It's been a real treat talking with you."

Her smile didn't so much as flicker. "If I could just mention this one thing before we agree on a day to meet."

"Why don't I call you after—"

"Air Waves is prepared to become a corporate sponsor for the Hailey Reyes Foundation. That sponsorship will include a sizable donation and free advertising. We like that a former national rodeo champion is now a champion for equestrian safety. Listeners like it, too."

She was an expert at pushing the right buttons.

"The day after tomorrow," Aaron said. "I'll meet you here. Late afternoon. Can you stick around that long?"

She positively glowed. And why not? Her mission was accomplished. "I need to meet with the executives of our station in Phoenix. I'll drive there tonight and return Monday afternoon. Is four o'clock all right?"

Alice came out the door and onto the porch. Her wandering glance lighted on Aaron. "Gary just called," she said. "He needs you down at the stables pronto."

"Excuse me." Aaron tipped his hat to Ms. Drummond. "I'll see you Monday."

She tilted her head appealingly. "I'm looking forward to it."

So was Aaron, which surprised him. He recalled Quick Draw's remark about seeing him soon and chuckled. The old coot knew all along Air Waves planned to make an offer.

Instead of heading down the porch steps and to the hitching rail where he'd left Dollar tied, Aaron went inside the main lodge, passed the tables displaying the silent-auction items and headed straight for the front desk.

He waited while Natalie finished with a guest who was leaving right after the ride and wanted to check out early.

"How was your cabin?" Natalie took his credit card and ran it through.

"Very nice. The view was great. My wife and I are hoping to come back Labor Day weekend."

"Be sure to reserve early. We're always full over the holidays." She handed him a pen and his receipt, which he signed.

Aaron lost himself in watching her work. Her fingers were quick and nimble at operating the computer keyboard and, he imagined, silky smooth when gliding over bare skin. *His* bare skin. The soft blond curls framing her face would look very appealing tousled after a night sleeping on his pillow.

"Hi." She beamed up at him.

When had the customer left?

Aaron cleared his throat. "I only have a minute. I have to get back to the stables."

"Actually, I think you have less than a minute. I heard Alice say my dad called."

Gary could wait. Aaron hadn't been this close to Natalie in nearly two weeks, and he wasn't going anywhere until he said…what? Damn, he might be able to think better if she wasn't staring at him with those thousand-watt baby blues.

"The ride is a spectacular success," she said, filling in the silence. "You did an incredible job."

"Everyone helped."

"Yes, but it was your hard work and your connections that really enabled us to pull it off. I can't wait for the silent auction tonight. Do you have any idea how much money you've raised so far?"

"Um…yes. Five thousand. No, six." Thinking was hard with her no farther away than the other side of the counter. He decided to give his brain a rest and say what was foremost on his mind. "Do you want to go out with me tonight?"

Her eyes went wide, which only enhanced their vivid color. "Like on a date?"

"Exactly like a date."

"Aaron." She lowered her voice. "I don't know if that's a good idea."

The hell with Jake or anyone else who might catch them. Aaron reached across the counter for Natalie's hand. "I'm not going to be here much longer. I want to spend every free minute I have with you."

She started to protest, but nothing came out of her mouth.

"Yes, seeing me will make it harder when I leave. Especially if we get along well, which I personally think is a foregone conclusion." He toyed with her fingers in the hopes of wearing down her resistance.

"I found a part-time nanny who's watching Shiloh today." She stared at their joined hands. "But I don't have a babysitter for tonight."

"We'll take her with us."

"Where?"

"I don't know. I'll think of something."

"You sure?" Natalie furrowed her brow. "She's a baby. Cries. Wets her diaper. Needs constant attention."

"I'm sure."

"You *would* have to say we could take her," she said resignedly.

"Is that a yes?"

"How can I refuse?"

Maybe he'd learned a little something about the art of persuasion from Ms. Drummond. "I'll come by your place after dinner to pick you up."

"Why don't we just leave together from the dining hall." Aaron had to ask. "And if Jake finds out?"

"He will. If he doesn't see us leave together, someone will tell him eventually."

"Gary called again," Alice hollered from her office doorway. "He said, and I quote, 'Aaron had better get his ass down here in the next five minutes or there'll be seven kinds of hell to pay.'"

"You'd better hurry," Natalie told Aaron and reclaimed her hands. "And don't worry about Jake. If he jumps to the wrong conclusion about us, I'll straighten him out tomorrow."

"What's the right conclusion?" Aaron asked.

"I guess we'll find out tonight."

The hint of promise in her voice filled him with the same sense of excitement bronc riding did. He hurried to where Dollar was tied up, wondering if Natalie realized the huge step she'd taken by agreeing to be seen with him.

It was only just beginning to dawn on him.

"YOU GO, GIRL." Alice flew out of her office, impressively agile in her inappropriate three-inch heels.

"What?" Natalie asked, intentionally distracted.

Alice skidded to a halt and rolled her eyes. "Oh, please. Your date with Aaron." She'd called him by his first name. Everyone did now, except Jake. It seemed her boss was the only one at Bear Creek Ranch who hadn't accepted Aaron's presence. A lot had changed in seven weeks. "I think I'm jealous."

Alice's excitement served to remind Natalie that she'd done something quite out of character. "I don't know what I was thinking."

"You would if you looked in the mirror. You've got it bad for him."

Natalie didn't need a mirror. Her insides had been fluttering nonstop since Aaron suggested—no, insisted—on taking her out tonight. And Shiloh. He hadn't hesitated one second when she'd mentioned her lack of a babysitter.

"He is good-looking," she mused.

"He's *gorgeous*. And he's got it bad for you, too."

"You think?"

"Quit playing dense."

Natalie smiled. "Maybe I just like hearing you say it."

People continued to pour into the lobby and file past the silent-auction display tables. Fortunately, no one came up to the front desk.

Alice nudged Natalie with her elbow. "I want to hear all the details tomorrow. Leave nothing out."

Natalie stared at Alice in amazement. She'd never seen her coworker act so…normal.

"There may not be any details worth mentioning. We're taking Shiloh with us."

"Trust me. If you're alone with Aaron, and you're bound to be at some point, there'll be details."

A shiver of anticipation went through Natalie at the prospect of her and Aaron being alone. Alice's next remark stopped it cold.

"Too bad he's only going to be here another week."

One week. Was she a fool to get involved with him? Or, a fool not to?

"I never figured you for having the guts to go against Jake," Alice said. "Got to tell you, I'm impressed."

"He won't like me seeing Aaron."

"There's nothing he can do about it. Not legally. The employee manual stipulates we can't fraternize with guests. Not one clause in there about owners or coworkers. I say go for it."

Natalie immediately began to wonder what "it" was and how much trouble with Jake "it" would get her into.

Chapter Thirteen

"Where are we going?" Natalie and Aaron walked out the dining-hall door and down the steps. "Do I need to change?"

He paused while he gave her a very lengthy, very thorough once-over. "No. You look great."

She smiled to herself. He hadn't really said whether her casual work clothes were appropriate or not. Had he even noticed? On the stone walkway, he offered to take Shiloh. Natalie marveled at how willingly she passed the carrier to him, how much she trusted him with her baby.

"You sure you don't mind missing the end of the auction?" she asked. When he'd invited her out, she forgot that the silent auction wouldn't be over until later that evening.

"There's no reason for me to be here. Alice has everything under control." The ground dropped suddenly at a steep angle, and he reached for her hand with his free one. "And she promised to call me on my cell phone with the final proceeds," he added.

Natalie should have guessed as much. From what she'd seen, Aaron left no stone unturned.

"Alice is quite the pistol."

"Yeah," Natalie agreed. She traveled this same walkway every day of her life and didn't need his assistance. But she gladly accepted it because she liked the sensation of Aaron's strong, sexy hand wrapped firmly around her fingers. "For a long while I wasn't sure I liked her very much. She can be kind of…standoffish. Lately, though, she's become a lot friendlier."

"How long has she worked here?"

"Going on six months."

"This ranch can have a real effect on people. Change them."

"Has it changed you?"

"In more ways than I thought possible."

Natalie could only guess at the meaning behind his subtle reference and wonder if it had anything to do with her.

They reached his truck in the parking lot. Natalie assumed they were heading into Payson or the family steak house down the road. He opened the passenger-side door and set Shiloh's carrier on the seat, then started to buckle it in.

"How far are we going?" she asked. The old truck didn't have a backseat, and she was uncomfortable with the idea of Shiloh riding in front. Even for short distances.

"Not far," he assured her.

"Maybe we should take my car."

Aaron snapped the seat belt in place, stepped back and unexpectedly bent to nuzzle Natalie's cheek. "Don't worry. We're not even leaving the ranch."

She resisted laying a hand over the spot where his lips had brushed her skin. Tossing the diaper bag on the truck floor, she climbed in.

Shiloh appeared content to go for a ride around the ranch. Fully awake and alert, she watched the two adults with interest. She seemed particularly fascinated by the turquoise bolo tie hanging from Aaron's rearview mirror.

"Where'd you learn to buckle in a carrier?"

"I have ten nieces and nephews. Number eleven is due in July."

"Wow. So many."

"That's what happens with six brothers and sisters."

"Are you close with them?"

"I haven't seen that much of them the last couple of years. I'm planning on staying a few days with my mom when I go back in a few weeks. Hopefully, everyone can come by while I'm there."

"Did they like Hailey? Sorry," she said a second later. "That's none of my business and rude of me to ask."

Aaron slung an arm over the back of the seat. His fingertips tickled the nape of Natalie's neck, giving her a small thrill. "As a matter of fact, they adored her. We visited the family I think four times while she and I were married."

Natalie observed Aaron from the corner of her eye. What would his many nosy siblings think of her? Would they disapprove of Aaron dating a woman with a baby by another man?

She put the questions from her mind. This was only their first date. No sense anticipating problems where there weren't any. "So, where are we going if we're not leaving the ranch?"

"You'll see."

"Ah. Being mysterious."

"More fun that way, don't you think?"

"Speak for yourself." She feigned annoyance.

He laughed, clearly seeing right through her pretense. "I thought we'd enjoy one of the ranch's more popular amenities."

"Horseback riding!" She was not taking Shiloh on a trail ride. Certainly not at night.

"Trust me. I want to see as much of you as I can this week. Not scare you off." They bumped along the old road, well below the ten-miles-an-hour posted limit.

"Hiking?"

He shook his head.

"ATVs?"

"Nope."

"That only leaves…"

He grinned.

She didn't. "You're not serious. Fishing with a five-month-old baby?"

"I have a plan."

"Hmm." She sat back and folded her arms across her waist.

"Olivia told me you like to fish."

"I do." She hadn't been since she was four months pregnant, too afraid she might slip on the wet rocks and hurt herself or the baby. "But it's not exactly an infant-friendly pastime."

"Wait and see." He removed his arm from behind the seat and patted her thigh.

Heat spread out from where his hand rested, warming Natalie from the inside out.

Fishing had never held such allure.

"I FOUND THIS SPOT a couple week ago when I had some free time." Aaron pulled off the dirt road he and Natalie had taken and parked beneath the overhanging branches of a tall oak tree. "There's a nice little pool formed by a bend in the creek."

"Near a patch of wild blackberry bushes," she added, pushing open the passenger-side door. "The berries won't be ripe for another month or two."

"Guess my secret spot's no secret." He went around to her side and helped her down.

"I've lived on this ranch my whole life. There aren't many spots I haven't fished."

Her smile caused his heart to give a quick kick.

"I brought a couple of folding lawn chairs. The bank's nice and flat."

Natalie removed the diaper bag from the floor of the truck and used her hip to slam shut the door. "It's a little late in the day. The trout in this creek don't bite much after dark."

He stopped unloading. "The great thing about fishing is that it's not all about catching fish." The light was too poor for him to discern her expression, but he did hear a slight intake of breath.

It was enough for now.

In the near distance, just beyond a stand of trees, the creek gurgled and splashed. While Natalie got the baby out of the truck, Aaron removed the fishing poles and other gear he'd packed earlier.

"There's no moon tonight." She stared at the sky.

Shiloh, wide awake, wiggled her small arms and legs.

"Not to worry." Aaron held up a kerosene lantern. "I came prepared."

"Me, too." Natalie patted the diaper bag. "Speaking of which…"

He lowered the tailgate. "Change her on this while I carry our stuff down."

By the time she finished with Shiloh, Aaron had everything unloaded. Together they wove through the trees and walked down the small incline to the creek bank.

"This is nice," Natalie said upon seeing their makeshift fishing camp.

He'd set up two folding chairs a safe distance from the bank. Between the two chairs was a small cooler containing cold drinks. The fishing poles and tackle box lay on the ground in front of the chairs, and the lantern hung from a tree branch.

"You got all this at the ranch?"

"We're well stocked. As the brochure says, the only necessity we don't provide is a fishing license."

"You have way too much free time if you're reading ranch brochures." Her laugh was low yet full of life.

He liked the sound of it, and mentally added laughter to the list of a hundred or so other things he liked about her.

"Thanks for bringing this." Natalie placed Shiloh's carrier on the small plastic tarp he'd brought and laid out beside one of the chairs.

"I didn't want to have to put her on the ground."

"I love fishing." Natalie bent and retrieved one of the poles, affording Aaron a dandy view of her jean-clad backside.

"It's one of my favorite sports, too," he muttered, his attention focused, his body stirring in response.

"Oh my gosh. I don't believe you brought this." She picked up a Sesame Street fishing pole and turned around. "I think Shiloh's still too young to hold this."

"Maybe not." Glad for the distraction, Aaron grabbed one

of the pole holders he'd brought and pushed it into the ground beside Shiloh.

"You're not serious."

"There's a pole holder for you, too, if you want."

"Then what would I do with my hands?"

So much for being distracted. "I'm sure we can come up with something."

"Like drinking soda?"

He swore he detected a hint of teasing in her tone. But it just might be his imagination running away with him.

"I'll bait the hooks," Aaron said. If he didn't get busy with fishing, he'd be tempted to get busy with something else entirely. "You grab us those sodas."

"Hey, I'm an avid fisherman, remember? I can bait my own hook."

"If you're that good, then bait Shiloh's pole and mine while you're at it."

They fished for nearly an hour with only a few nibbles to show for their efforts. Aaron didn't care. He enjoyed talking to Natalie. When Shiloh started to cry, Natalie excused herself and went to the truck. He recalled his first day on the ranch when he'd walked into Jake's office and discovered her nursing Shiloh. Tonight, like then, he saw nothing, but his mind nonetheless conjured an image.

What he felt about that image had little to do with sex and a lot to do with his longing for a wife and family. When he'd first lost Hailey, he couldn't conceive of making a life with another woman. Eventually, his grief lessened, but he still didn't view the women he met as potential love interests.

Until Natalie.

"I had two job offers recently," he said when she returned. "Well, one serious offer. The other could turn into something serious if I pursue it."

"Rodeoing?" She held Shiloh against her shoulder and rubbed her back. The baby looked ready to drop off any second.

"No. Believe it or not, they're both in the media. One television, one, the serious offer, in radio."

"Why wouldn't I believe it? You used to be on that cable rodeo show and have done, what, three broadcasts with KRDS?"

He chuckled. "I guess it still surprises me that I wound up in broadcasting. It was never my goal. I'm just a cowboy."

"Would either of the jobs take you away from the foundation?"

Natalie had resettled Shiloh in the carrier and was fussing over her, adjusting the blanket just so. She was a good mother. Another one of the hundred or so things he liked about her. And she could bait a hook like a pro.

"That's the really nice part," he said. "I'd only have to work a few days a week. The bad part is I'd have to be on the road those days."

"I wouldn't mind traveling now and again."

"This from a girl who lives at the same place she works."

"You'd probably be shocked to learn I can count on ten fingers the number of times I've visited Phoenix. And I've never been out of Arizona."

He *was* shocked. "Where would you go if you could pick anyplace in the world?"

"Hawaii." She sighed wistfully. "On a cruise. For two weeks."

"Cruise? Are you afraid of flying?"

"Don't know." She shrugged. "I haven't ever done it."

"Then why the cruise? And why two weeks?"

"Because for once in my life I want people to wait on me. Pick up after me. Bring me my food. Listen to my complaints and bend over backward to ensure that I'm happy."

"You've thought a lot about this."

"For years." She removed her pole from the holder and tested the line. "But no matter where I went, I'd always come home to Bear Creek Ranch. There's no place I'd rather live."

"Tell me about Drew."

Frowning, she fiddled with her reel. "I'd rather talk about Hawaii."

"He must have had some redeeming qualities."

"I thought so once. That was before he asked to abdicate his rights to Shiloh."

"Why would he do that?"

"Besides the fact he's a jerk?" She returned her pole to the holder.

"I can understand parents don't always get along and have to split up. But to abandon your kid?"

"I think his new wife is behind it. She isn't keen on their baby having an older half sister."

"They have a baby?"

"About to."

Jerk was right. Drew hadn't wasted any time hooking up with another woman.

Aaron reached for Natalie's hand. "That must be really hard on you."

"It's for the best," she said resolutely. "Drew doesn't deserve Shiloh." They sat in silence for a few minutes, both of them staring at the black water rushing past. "I'm not saying death is better than being dumped by a loser like Drew. But you loved Hailey, and you cherish your memories of her. If you'd had children, you could have told them about how wonderful their mother was. I don't know what to tell Shiloh." Natalie glanced down at her sleeping baby.

"When it's time, the right thing will come to you."

"I hope so."

"Hailey and I almost had a child."

"You did?"

"She was pregnant when she died."

"Oh, Aaron," Natalie gasped and gripped his hand. "I'm so sorry."

"I didn't tell anybody at the time of the accident. I was having enough trouble coping as it was. I finally told Jake a few weeks ago. He took it hard."

"I can imagine." Her voice was thick with emotion. "How awful for everyone. You, especially." She lifted his hand to her cheek. It was damp from her tears.

Aaron felt one more crack in his heart heal. Without conscious thought, he leaned toward her. She did the same.

Their lips no sooner touched then a sharp click sounded, followed by a loud whirring.

She drew back with a start. "What's that?"

Had it been any other interruption, Aaron might have been annoyed. Instead, he laughed.

"I think your daughter just landed her first fish."

Chapter Fourteen

Natalie didn't suffer a single moment of indecision while Aaron walked her to her front door. She was going to kiss him goodnight. If he didn't make the first move, she would.

He'd been right about them only having a week to figure out if what they had going between them was worth fighting the many obstacles facing them, only one of which was Jake. Aaron's potential new job was perhaps the most difficult obstacle. Relationships tended to suffer from frequent periods of separation.

One step at a time, she told herself. First, the good-night kiss.

She hadn't counted on a sleeping baby in a carrier and a cumbersome diaper bag getting in the way of intimacy. She wanted both her arms free to wrap around Aaron.

He unwittingly obliged. "Here, I'll hold Shiloh while you get the door."

"Thanks."

He took the carrier from her, and she dug her key out of her pants pocket. Bear Creek Ranch was a safe place to live, but as a single mother with a baby, Natalie took no chances. Unfortunately, more than one cabin had been broken into or vandalized by juveniles.

"Thanks for tonight," she said, unlocking the door. "I had a great time even though I was outfished by my daughter."

"Great enough to go out with me tomorrow night?"

She stuffed the key back in her pocket, opened the door and looked back over her shoulder at him. "Why don't you come inside, and we'll talk about it."

Enough light shone through the open door for her to clearly see his face. What wasn't clear to her were the emotions flitting across it.

"You need to know something first."

"What's that?"

His seriousness caused her to doubt herself. Had she come on too strong? Put him in an awkward position? Given him the wrong idea? The diaper bag on her shoulder suddenly weighed a hundred pounds.

"If I'm alone with you in your cabin, I'm going to kiss you."

Her exhale of relief came out as a shudder of anticipation. She remembered what he'd said about kissing her that day they were in the employee dining area. *Going to*, not try. He'd said it again tonight with the same conviction.

"I'm counting on it." Taking Shiloh from him, she stepped inside.

He followed and stopped her in the middle of the living room with a hand on her arm. "Here. Alone with you. I might not be able to stop at just a kiss." His grip on her arm melted into a caress that grew increasingly bolder. "I haven't been with a woman since Hailey. I haven't wanted to until now."

She swallowed and hoped he didn't notice her trembling hands. "I haven't been with a man since Drew," she said softly. "And he was the only one."

Aaron groaned, low and ragged. "Maybe we should rethink this kiss. I don't want to take advantage of you."

If not for Shiloh, Natalie might have gone into his arms. "You always say the right thing."

"I'm not trying to." He removed his cowboy hat and raked a hand through his hair. "You'd tell me to get lost if you heard what I really want to say."

"I might not. I might be thinking the same thing." She started toward Shiloh's bedroom. "Wait here while I put her to bed. Help yourself to whatever's in the fridge. When I get done, we'll talk more about that kiss."

Shiloh cooperated by not waking up while Natalie changed her diaper and dressed her in a sleeper. Fishing and being outside all evening had thrown them both off schedule. She doubted Shiloh would sleep her usual six hours straight through.

Nuzzling a satiny cheek, Natalie laid Shiloh in the bassinet. Her daughter was growing so fast. Soon, next week probably, she'd have to buy a crib. When she reached over to adjust the night-light, she was startled to find Aaron standing in the doorway studying her.

For a moment, neither of them moved. It had been a long time since a man desired her and made that desire known. She wanted to savor the sensation a while longer.

"I hope I wasn't intruding," he said.

"It's all right."

"You're incredibly beautiful."

Her hand went automatically to her hair. "After working all day and fishing tonight, I must be a mess."

"Anything but." His gaze was hot and unwavering.

She went to him, her eyes never leaving his face.

"Are you sure, *querida?*" He pulled her out into the hallway. "Because once we start, there's no stopping. No going back."

"My whole world is this ranch."

"I know. And I don't want you to jeopardize your place here because of me."

"You don't understand." She lifted a hand and skimmed her knuckles across his bristled jawline. "I live here. I work here. I spend most of my free time here." Her fingers glided down the column of his neck and dipped beneath the collar of his shirt. He tensed at the slight but potent contact. "I want you to take me places tonight I've never been, show me things I've never seen. Excite me in ways I never dreamed possible."

A groan came from deep in his chest. He lowered his head for that kiss they'd been talking so much about.

"Not here." She slipped away from him.

He hesitated.

"What is it?" she asked.

"I wasn't counting on…this. I don't have any protection with me."

She smiled, pleased that he hadn't assumed their date would automatically end with them in bed together. "I have some in the bathroom drawer." She started to explain the condoms were left over from when she and Drew were together, but decided she'd brought up his name enough for one evening. The next few hours belonged to her and Aaron alone.

Refusing to turn on the bathroom light and ruin the seductive mood, she fumbled in the dark, finally locating the condoms in the back of the drawer. Together, they went into the bedroom. She was acutely aware of him in the darkness. The rustle of his clothing. The muffled thud of his boots on her carpeted floor. His uneven breathing, so like her own.

She removed a condom from the box and set both on the nightstand. If she had known ahead of time they'd wind up here, she would have put candles out. Aaron by flickering candlelight would be worth seeing.

She sensed him behind her and turned. In the next instant, she was where she'd wanted to be all evening. In his arms.

No sooner did his tongue touch her lips than she parted them, her soft moan encouraging him to sample every corner of her mouth. This kiss wasn't like the one on her porch steps and definitely not like the practically chaste one in the employee dining area. No, this kiss was pure heat, pure hunger, pure passion.

One of his hands found the small of her back and pulled her flush against him. The hard ridge of his erection pressed into the junction of her legs, and she went weak from a sudden surge of pleasure. Sighing, she reached up to sift her fingers through his hair. It was thick and softer than she'd expected. Her leg wound around his calf, bringing them into even closer contact.

He broke away from her only to lower his head and tantalize the sensitive spot beneath her ear with his tongue. Simultaneously, his hand yanked at her shirt. The fabric stuck in the waistband of her jeans and seemed to defeat him. He uttered a desperate curse and yanked harder.

She stepped back. "Wait."

"Sorry," he said in a strained voice. "I got carried away."

"No. That's not it." With trembling fingers, she pulled her shirt from her pants and over her head, then tossed it on the floor. "You were taking too long."

"I'm out of practice," he said and drew her to him again.

His worn work shirt rubbing against her bra gave her goose bumps. She wondered how his bare skin would feel on hers. He must have been wondering the same thing, too, for he tugged at the snaps of his shirt, freeing them one by one. Each pop heightened Natalie's anticipation. No sooner did he have the shirt unfastened than she helped him out of it. His undershirt came next. Then her bra.

His skin was warm, almost feverish. The muscles of his back and shoulders were corded and powerful. She would have kept exploring the contours of his muscled frame all night, but he apparently had other plans.

He cupped her breast and ran the pad of his thumb over her nipple. It instantly formed a tight bud. She moaned her enjoyment only to gasp when a small amount of breast milk leaked out.

"I…ah…" Embarrassed, she tried to push his hand away.

He wouldn't let her. "So sweet," he murmured and continued to rub her damp nipple with his thumb. Then, to her shock and intense enjoyment, he lowered his head and licked the moisture from her.

"Aaron." Her knees went weak when his mouth grew bolder and his caresses hotter. Her need, great to begin with, intensified.

Without warning, he straightened, unfastening his belt buckle as he did. Seconds later, she heard the zipper of his jeans.

He kicked off his boots and shed the remainder of his clothes. Her hands went right to him and discovered he was entirely naked.

What she wouldn't give for those candles now.

He didn't wait for her to undress, and finished the job himself, unbuttoning her jeans and sliding them down her legs. When he finished, they found the bed and tumbled onto it, a glorious tangle of arms and legs. He rolled her onto her back, pinning her to the mattress and bringing their antics to a tantalizing halt.

She couldn't see his eyes in the dark but imagined they were boring into hers. Impulsively, she reached up and traced the contours of his face with her fingers. When her hand ventured close to his mouth, he turned his head and kissed her palm.

"I care about you, *querida*. I wouldn't be here if I didn't."

She believed him. "I care about you, too." As soon as she said the words, she realized she could easily feel a whole lot more for him.

Aaron's hands roamed her body, touching and teasing. Lowering his head to her breast, he tasted her again. When the sensation became unbearable, she arched her back and pleaded with him to stop.

He did, by moving his mouth lower.

To the valley between her breasts. Down the flat expanse of her belly. Lower still. Parting her legs, he kissed the insides of her thighs. That was only the beginning.

Fulfilling her earlier request, he took her to places she'd never been and excited her in ways she never dreamed possible.

Natalie's climax rocked them both. Granted, her experience was limited, but this went beyond her wildest expectations. It was an experience she wanted to reciprocate. When he'd settled beside her, she closed her hand around his erection.

"Lie back," she told him, stroking his hard length.

"No." Aaron gently disengaged her hand.

"But—"

"Later." He grabbed the condom off the nightstand. "If you try that now, I won't last. And I want to be inside you." He tore open the condom and put it on. "Deep inside."

Her cry of delight when he entered her was cut short by his mouth claiming hers. She lifted her hips, accepted him fully. He responded by increasing the rhythm of his thrusts. When he came moments later, her legs were entwined with his, her arms clutching him to her and her heart forever lost to him.

AT THE FIRST TINY WAIL, Aaron sat bolt upright in bed. *Natalie's bed.* They must have fallen asleep. He shouldn't be surprised. They'd made love twice, the second time slow and infinitely more satisfying. Afterward, they'd talked for at least an hour, mostly about their families and the ranch. Him getting up and returning to his bunkhouse never entered the conversation.

In the course of one evening, Natalie went from being someone with whom Aaron shared a strong attraction to a necessary part of his life. Staying away from her for the remainder of his stint at the ranch wouldn't be possible.

Leaving at the end of next week might not be, either.

"She's probably hungry," Natalie said groggily and climbed out of bed. "I'll be right back."

He heard her stumbling around in the dark, a closet door opening and closing. "Can I help?"

She was putting something on. A bathrobe? "Go back to sleep," she whispered.

Shiloh's wailing intensified.

"What time is it?" Aaron sat up and swung his legs over the side of the bed.

"Early. Really early." She kissed the top of his head and padded down the hall to Shiloh's room.

He leaned over and groped in the dark for his pants. Removing his cell phone from its carrying case, he checked the time. Three twenty-six. Early indeed. He didn't have to be at the stables for another two hours.

The idea of going back to bed appealed to him. Three and

a half hours of sleep wasn't enough, not with a full day of work ahead of him. Add to that all the extra work cleaning up after the breakfast trail ride.

If he went back to bed, however, he'd miss spending every spare moment with Natalie. The choice was an easy one.

Tugging on his jeans and nothing else, he followed a dim light to the second bedroom. Natalie sat in a rocker by the cradle, nursing Shiloh and humming softly.

Longing pulled hard inside his chest, so incredibly powerful and yet so basic. A woman to love and a child of his own. He'd wanted that for years. Thought he had it with Hailey, only to be denied. Then Natalie came into his life and with her, Shiloh. The acute emptiness he'd lived with for the past two years was no more.

Would it return when he left Bear Creek Ranch?

He wished he didn't have to go. At least not so soon. Longing warred with responsibility and the latter won.

"I have to spend a week in Phoenix," he said, approaching her. "Maybe longer. Take care of some foundation business that can't be put off. Then I'll come back to the ranch."

He stood beside the rocker and gazed down at her. Natalie didn't show the least bit of embarrassment, not even when he lifted the flap of her bathrobe in order to see better. The thoughts and feelings running through him weren't sexual in nature but rather something much stronger and far less fleeting.

"Come back permanently?" she asked in a low voice.

He dropped to one knee and rested a hand on Shiloh's head. What little hair she had was blond and curly. Like her mother's. She sucked lustily, her eyes flitting from Aaron to Natalie and back to him.

"That will depend on a lot of things," he murmured, absently rubbing Shiloh's head.

"Such as?"

He thought Natalie might intentionally be keeping her tone casual. "My meeting tomorrow afternoon with the gal from Air Waves Communications."

"Are you going to take the job?"

"I have to do something. I've been kicking around too long now. Resting on past laurels."

"I wouldn't call the foundation kicking around."

"Don't get me wrong. The foundation's important. But I'm finally ready to crawl out of the hole I've been hiding in. I have you to thank for that. And this ranch." He chuckled. "Funny. I didn't want to come here. Wouldn't have if not for my accountant and her endless prodding." His hand abandoned Shiloh's head to stroke Natalie's cheek. "I'm glad I did."

She covered his hand with her free one, the look in her eyes tender. "Me, too."

"Can I see you again tonight?"

"I'd love to hear how the silent auction went. And more about your job offers."

"Maybe we can ditch the ranch and head into Payson. Find a nice, kid-friendly restaurant."

"You don't mind taking her?" Natalie shifted Shiloh to her other breast.

"Remember the ten, soon to be eleven, nieces and nephews? You're not a Reyes if you don't like kids."

Her smile belied the trace of sadness in her eyes. "I didn't know if it would be difficult on you being around a baby after losing yours."

"It's not." If anything, Natalie and Shiloh made his loss easier to bear. "Will she go back to sleep when she's finished?"

Shiloh's eyelids were drooping and she'd lost interest in nursing.

Natalie propped her upright and patted her back. "She usually does."

"Come back to bed afterward." He brushed a flyaway hair from her face, tucking it behind her ear.

She leaned into his hand and made a small sound of contentment.

Shiloh promptly burped.

"Let me change her," Natalie said. "I won't be long."

Stretched out in bed, Aaron waited for her. He kept mentally replaying the last part of their conversation. Being with her and Shiloh did erase his loneliness. Was that the entire basis of his feelings for them? Could he be substituting them for the wife and child he'd lost?

When Natalie joined him in bed, the feelings she evoked were fresh and entirely different from those he'd had for his late wife. When she straddled his hips and began to make incredible love to him, the nagging questions all but disappeared.

They returned later, however, and came back to haunt him again and again at unexpected times throughout the day.

Chapter Fifteen

"You missed a spot."

"Did I?" Natalie doubted it but let Aaron dry her naked back anyway. She liked the sensation of his hands on her, and when he'd finished wiping off the last drops of water, imaginary or real, she smiled contentedly. "Thanks."

His arms went around her waist and pulled her snug against him. "Anytime."

He didn't appear in a rush to get dressed and ready for work. Neither was she.

It was hard for her to believe that a whole seven days had passed with them waking up side by side, showering together and grabbing a quick cup of coffee before leaving for the dining hall and breakfast. She could easily imagine him toweling her dry every day for the rest of her life.

Natalie cautioned herself to go easy with the forever-and-ever thoughts about Aaron. They hadn't discussed the future or what would happen when he left. Her fault. Whenever he brought up the subject, she changed it, not wanting to put a damper on their remaining time together.

The inevitable could be postponed for only so long. As his remaining days on the ranch dwindled, reality set in, and their need to talk couldn't be ignored. But, oh, the last week had been so nice. If only they could go on like they were for just a few more days.

He bent his head and nuzzled her neck. At the brush of his warm lips on her cool skin, shivers went through her. She stared at their reflections in the small mirror over the bathroom sink. The sight of his dark hair and tanned complexion beside her considerably fairer features made an evocative picture. If she didn't have to wake Shiloh soon and get her ready for the babysitter, Natalie might be inclined to take Aaron back to bed.

"I'll start the coffee," he said and released her to hang his towel over the shower-curtain rod.

No longer distracted by his caresses, Natalie's mind returned to their talk and the necessity for it. "I'll be out in a minute." She had no intention of discussing their future while standing naked in the bathroom.

"The gal from Air Waves called me again yesterday," Aaron said ten minutes later when they were in the kitchen.

"Have you decided to accept their job offer?" Here it was, the perfect opening.

"I'm leaning that way." He sat at the dining table, his legs stretched out. "I wanted to discuss it with you first."

"Me?"

"I'd be traveling several days a week. The question is, where do I spend the rest of the week?"

She slid into the chair next to him. Striving for nonchalance, she asked, "Where do you want to spend it?"

"Here. With you. I figured you knew that."

"I wasn't sure," she admitted shyly.

"What about you? Where do you want me to stay on my off days?"

The slight unsteadiness in his voice brought a smile to her lips. He was always so strong and confident. Seeing that trace of insecurity endeared him to her all the more.

"Here, too," she reassured him. "But that's a problem."

"Jake."

Her boss, and his dislike of Aaron, was the main reason she'd avoided this conversation all week.

"Not just him. My employment contract stipulates that no one other than Shiloh can live with me."

Her contract actually stipulated that only spouses and children could live with her. She wasn't ready to suggest Aaron and she get married just so he had a place to stay. Although the idea of marrying him had crossed her mind once or twice this past week…

"I'll buy a place nearby. I saw some houses for sale on the road between the ranch and Payson."

She laughed. "You can't just go out and buy a house."

"Why not?"

"Houses are expensive."

"I have money."

"No, you d— You do?"

"And more if I take the job with Air Waves. Their offer's pretty generous. Why?" He cracked a grin. "Did you think I was broke?"

"Kind of." Her cheeks warmed with embarrassment.

In hindsight, it had been silly of her to assume he was without resources just because he drove an old truck and trailer. Aaron had demonstrated his excellent business skills repeatedly and ran a successful foundation. He likely handled his personal finances with the same finesse.

"Okay," she relented. "You can buy a house. Wouldn't something closer to Phoenix or Flagstaff make more sense, seeing as you'll have to travel so much? We're two hours from the closest airport."

"Phoenix and Flagstaff aren't near you. I'm willing to drive if that's what it takes."

Quite a sacrifice he was making for her, one that called for a similar sacrifice from her in return. Was she willing?

Absolutely. Aaron was everything she wanted in a man, and she'd be a fool to let him walk out of her life.

"That leaves Jake." Having committed to giving permanence with Aaron a try, she was eager to move ahead.

"You know, it's funny."

"What?" She got up from the table and went to the counter to shut off the coffeemaker and rinse out the pot.

"That Jake hasn't said anything to us. One of the employees must have told him by now."

"Maybe we've misjudged him, and he's okay with the idea of us dating."

"I'm more inclined to think he's gathering his forces."

So was Natalie. Every time Jake had buzzed her to come into his office this past week, she'd instantly frozen, afraid he was going to demand she stop seeing Aaron.

Aaron put his empty mug in the dishwasher. "I'll talk to him today."

"I'll go with you."

"I think I should do this alone."

Like Natalie would let that happen. "I know him better than you do. And I'm used to his temper."

Aaron shook his head. "His problem isn't with you, it's with me. If you were dating someone else, he wouldn't care."

She stood in front of him, hands on her hips. "This involves me, too. I won't be excluded."

"Did I ever tell you I have a thing for bossy women?"

"That's good or we'd be in real trouble."

"Okay. You win." He swept her into an embrace, taking her by surprise, and rested his chin atop her head. "Is Jake going to be in his office this afternoon?"

"I'll check and call you if he isn't."

"Teresa can handle the last trail ride for me." He kissed Natalie on the forehead. "I'll meet you in the lobby around four."

"Okay," she said, her enthusiasm abruptly fading and anxiety taking its place.

If only her boss weren't so unpredictable lately, she'd feel more at ease.

"GOODBYE, ELLEN," Natalie said in a falsely chipper voice.

There was no response.

Both she and Alice turned their heads to watch Jake's ex-wife breeze past them, then exchanged raised eyebrows. The door to his office had not been closed, allowing Natalie and Alice to hear bits and pieces of the conversation—make that heated discussion—that had transpired the last ten minutes.

Both women breathed a little easier once Ellen was gone.

"Good riddance," Alice muttered softly and slipped into her office.

Evidently, she'd decided to wait a while before presenting Jake with the monthly reports, not that Natalie blamed her. She checked her watch, something she'd been doing every few minutes. Aaron was due momentarily for his talk with Jake. She wished he wasn't coming on the heels of Ellen's visit.

The thought was barely formed when her intercom buzzed, giving her a start.

"Natalie, can you come in here a minute?"

"Sure, Jake." She picked up a stack of e-mails she'd printed out earlier, well aware she was taking them along with her as a potential distraction tactic. "What's up," she asked, sitting in one of the chairs.

"I'm okay," Jake said.

"What?"

"Quit giving me the mother-hen stare." His voice sounded tired but not angry.

"Sorry." She shuffled the e-mails in her lap. "I couldn't help hearing you and Ellen earlier. Everything all right?"

He rubbed his forehead. "She's going on a trip in a couple weeks with Travis. To some resort in Cabo San Lucas. She needs me to watch the girls while they're gone."

"Wow." Natalie wasn't sure how to respond.

"I gave her a hard time about the short notice but the truth is, I'm thrilled to have the girls to myself for ten days. I just wish she wasn't going with her boyfriend. The girls don't like him much and apparently threw a fit when Ellen told them about the trip."

Natalie watched the scowl on Jake's face deepen and quickly

utilized her plan B. "I thought you might like to look at these," she said and handed over the e-mails.

All of them were from guests who'd attended the breakfast ride, expressing their thanks for the hospitality shown them and raving about what a good time they'd had. Many promised to return the following year or to visit the ranch for a lengthier stay in the near future.

"Hailey would be very proud of you, Jake," she said when he was done reading.

"For what?"

"The ride and the money raised. I heard the total came to over seventy-five hundred dollars."

"I had very little to do with that," he said, his tone dismissive. "It was all Aaron's doing."

"Don't sell yourself short. Without your support and your contacts in the community, he couldn't have pulled off an event of such enormous size in so short a period of time."

"That's debatable."

Natalie wanted to jump up and strangle her boss. If only he could get past his animosity toward Aaron and see what a great team they made, how their individual abilities and talents complemented each other. Maybe then she wouldn't constantly feel as if she had to chose between them.

It was, she decided, a lost cause. Jake's opinion of Aaron had been formed back when his much-adored little sister left to go on the road with her rodeo-champion husband. Nothing had happened since then to change his mind, not even a wildly successful breakfast ride.

"Is there anything else you need?" she asked. "I have to get back to the front desk."

"There is. I was considering revamping our weekend package deals."

"Oh, okay."

For several minutes they discussed cabins and amenities and bundling them together at a discounted rate. Natalie had trouble staying focused. Her attention kept wandering back to Aaron and his impending arrival.

"I'll update our Web site in the next day or two," she said once they'd settled on specifics. "What about using excerpts from some of the e-mails and letters as endorsements?"

"Good idea."

Thinking that was all, Natalie started to rise.

"There is one more thing."

Responding to the change of tone in Jake's voice, she slowly lowered herself into her chair. Here it was, the confrontation she'd been dreading all week.

"I'm not sure how to approach this so I'll just come right out and say it."

"This sounds serious." She tried to lighten the sudden tension with a laugh.

What was left of Jake's former smile thinned. "Your personal life is your own. I have no business telling you what to do."

"Not entirely my own," she admitted. "I do live on your ranch and in one of your cabins." She'd been breaking company policy by allowing Aaron to spend the last six nights with her. If Jake reprimanded her for the infraction, she deserved it. "Being my employer does give you a few rights."

"I'm also your friend. I've watched you grow up and change from a shy kid to a confident, capable woman who contributes significantly to the operation of this ranch."

"Thank you, Jake."

"I hate seeing friends make mistakes."

"Aaron isn't a mistake."

"I'll be the first to admit I don't like the two of you dating. But as Carolina frequently reminds me, there's nothing I can or should do about it." He momentarily averted his gaze. When he next spoke, she understood the reason for his embarrassment. "Ellen told me he's been sleeping over at your place. She sees his truck in the mornings when she drives by."

Natalie hadn't heard that part of Jake's argument with his ex-wife. "I should have said something," she offered lamely.

"I can quote company policy and tell you he can't stay with you again, but I won't. Rules and regulations aren't the reason you need to end your relationship with him."

"I beg your pardon?" Natalie's irritation flared. She'd expected a lecture from the Jake who was like an older brother to her or a reprimand from the Jake who was her boss. Not a directive.

"I don't want to see you hurt again."

"I appreciate your concern. But Aaron isn't like Drew."

"No, he's not. He's famous."

"What does that have to do with anything?"

"It's easy to get swept up in the excitement of dating a celebrity. Especially for someone who's vulnerable and inexperienced."

"Don't confuse me with your sister."

"I'm not," he said, his jaw tensing.

"I wouldn't blame you if you did. Our situations do appear alike on the surface. But they're not. For starters, I'm not rushing into anything. And Aaron isn't the same man who married Hailey. He's changed since then."

Her point, which seemed logical to her, appeared lost on Jake. If anything, he became angrier.

"He's leaving. Or have you forgotten that?"

"He'll be back."

"In a year."

"In a month at the most. Hopefully less."

"Is that what he told you?"

"It's what he promised."

Jake made a sound of disgust. "He's a user, Natalie. A manipulator. He ruined Hailey's life. Took her away from everything and everyone she knew and loved. Is that what you want, too?"

"Who said anything about—"

"I'm not taking her away from here," Aaron answered on Natalie's behalf.

He stood in the office doorway, one hand braced on the

jamb, his hat pulled low over his eyes. She and Jake must had been too engrossed in their conversation to hear the bell over the lobby entrance chime.

Natalie's heart gave a small leap at the sight of Aaron. She was glad to see him and also worried. This wasn't how she'd imagined his conversation with Jake going.

"Butt out, Reyes." Jake glowered at Aaron.

"The hell I will." Aaron stepped into the office, his stride that of a man on a mission.

Jake stood.

Natalie's glance traveled from one man to the other. Once again, she felt as if she was standing in the middle of a lonely railroad track with two speeding locomotives approaching from opposite directions.

Only this time, she had no intention of dodging the crash by taking a shortcut home.

THE SOFT THUD of Aaron's boots on the wooden floor helped to ground him and keep his temper in check. Losing it might make him feel better, but wouldn't help Natalie. And she was his main concern.

She rose and faced him, her smile nervous and, at the same time, brave.

"There's no reason for Natalie to leave Bear Creek Ranch," Aaron said calmly. "I'm going to extend my stay another week and be back again around mid-May."

"No." The word exploded from Jake's mouth. "Your eight weeks are up."

"You don't have the authority to refuse me. That would require a vote."

"Do you honestly think my family will take your side over mine?"

"I don't need their permission. I'll rent a cabin and pay full rate if I have to. But I'm coming back."

"Management reserves the right to refuse to rent to anyone," Jake said. "And I'm management."

Aaron was tired of arguing. From the very beginning, his relationship with Jake had been strained and difficult. "Isn't it time we put the past behind us?"

"Kind of hard when you keep shoving it in my face."

Here was one downside of the breakfast trail ride Aaron hadn't considered. The constant reminder of his late wife and the old hurts associated with her death. "The foundation does a lot of good. Hailey would be—"

Jake didn't let him finish. "You haven't changed your M.O. one bit, Reyes."

"Meaning what?"

"Two months. Isn't that how long you knew Hailey before you two eloped? Now Natalie. You're right on schedule. Another woman from Bear Creek Ranch falls victim to your charms."

Screw maintaining his temper. "That's enough!" Aaron shouted.

"I won't let you hurt her!" Jake shouted back. "I couldn't stop Hailey from going off with you but I can Natalie."

"Carolina's right." Natalie leaped to her feet. "You're over-stepping your bounds."

Jake came out from behind his desk. "If you persist in seeing Aaron, I won't renew your employment contract when it comes up in four months. If he spends even one more night at your place, I'll fire you on the spot."

She stared at him in disbelief, her eyes filling with tears. "You wouldn't."

"Only to protect you."

"I don't need protection. Not from Aaron."

"You don't know him like I do."

"No, I know him better."

Few people possessed the nerve to stand up to Jake. Aaron wasn't about to let Natalie do it alone and went to stand by her.

"He's bluffing. Trying to scare you. He won't fire you."

"I don't bluff, as you well know," Jake said.

"It's me you have a quarrel with. Not Natalie. There's no reason to involve her."

"You're right. Leave Bear Creek Ranch tomorrow, and her job's safe."

"You can't force him to leave," Natalie cried, wiping her cheeks. "I won't let you."

"I'll do whatever it takes to get him off Bear Creek Ranch and away from you."

Aaron stepped in front of Natalie. "You son of a bitch. Do you have any idea what you're doing? She's the best damn employee you've got *and* your friend."

"If you're not gone by tomorrow, she'll be somebody else's employee."

Natalie had told Aaron that Jake was capable of, even good at, separating the ranch from his personal life. She'd been wrong. To carry out his grudge against Aaron, Jake was willing to ruin her life. Could he sink any lower?

"I don't deserve this, Jake," Natalie whispered.

"You're right, you don't. I hate holding any kind of hammer over your head." It seemed as if the anger burning within him died, leaving sadness in its wake. "But how else do I make you realize he's not the man you deserve any more than Drew was?"

In that instant, Aaron understood Jake in a way he never thought possible. His ex-brother-in-law had lost his sister, first to Aaron, then to death. His wife left him for somebody else. His daughters no longer lived with him. And now Natalie, whom he cared for greatly, was, to his way of thinking, betraying him with the same man who'd taken his sister from him.

"Aaron." Natalie reached for his hand. "Take me home."

There was nothing else he wanted more.

"Come back here." Jake lowered his voice. "Please."

She stopped at the door. "It's almost quitting time. If you're going to fire me for leaving ten minutes early, then do it. Otherwise, I'll talk to you in the morning."

Aaron guided her through the lobby and out the door. Alice, who sat at Natalie's workstation, gave them a small parting wave.

"I'm sorry for everything," Aaron said once they were outside.

"It's okay." She smiled through her tears. "Despite what he said, Jake won't fire me."

"I don't know. He seemed pretty convincing to me."

She looked up at him so sweetly, so trustingly, Aaron couldn't help but believe everything was going to eventually resolve itself. They went behind the building to where her golf cart was parked.

"What if he doesn't renew your contract?"

"It won't come to that."

It definitely wouldn't if Aaron left and didn't return after the foundation board meeting. "Jake can be stubborn. You might be out of a job."

"I'll find another one." Some of her bravado deserted her.

"And you'll lose your home."

She swallowed. "We'll have your new house. It's about time I got out on my own. Experienced more of life away from the ranch."

Aaron should be happy. She'd chosen him over Jake. Instead, he felt sick. This wasn't right. Natalie shouldn't have to sacrifice everything that was dear to her in order for them to be together.

Like Hailey did.

For a moment, the past and present mingled together, confusing Aaron. Two women, Hailey and Natalie. Both of them in a lifelong relationship with Jake, both of them willing to end it and abandon the only home they'd ever known for Aaron.

Why did it always have to come down to this?

Chapter Sixteen

"You're leaving," Natalie said flatly.

"First thing in the morning."

Aaron's admission confirmed what she already knew. She'd seen it in his eyes during the drive to her cabin from the main lodge. Heard it in his voice. Sensed it in his withdrawal even now as they sat together on her front-porch steps discussing the scene in Jake's office. She had experience, after all, when it came to men deserting her and recognized the signs. What she lacked was a shield against the pain.

This time it hurt infinitely worse. She hadn't seriously contemplated quitting her job and moving away from her home for Drew.

"I'm sorry." Aaron put an arm around her shoulders.

She stiffened. How could she cuddle with someone who was about to shatter her world?

"You said you were going to stay another week."

"That was before Jake threatened to fire you."

"I told you, no way will the rest of the Tuckers let him."

"Jake doesn't need their vote."

"But he needs their support and their love. Whatever differences they have, they're family and dependent on each other for their livelihood." She pressed her steepled fingers to her lips. She and Aaron had been so happy this past week. Only this morning, they were making plans for the future. All that changed in a matter of minutes. "Jake's just mad. He'll be over it by tomorrow. You'll see."

"I can't take the chance."

"Will you come back in May?" She was aware of the desperation in her voice and hated it.

"I don't know yet."

He didn't invite her to come see him or offer to call her, and she wasn't about to ask. Her heart couldn't withstand another crushing blow.

She instinctively scooted away from Aaron. He countered her efforts by locking his arm around her.

"I'm not one to give up so easily, Natalie. And anyone who tries to run my life learns pretty quickly they can't. But Jake changed the rules when he brought you into it."

"I think we should talk to my parents. Dad has a lot of influence with Jake and Mom's in business with Millie."

"I don't want to involve them. Knowing your dad, he'd do something drastic like quit his job to save yours."

"You're probably right." Natalie had a sudden glimmer into what Aaron must be thinking and feeling, the awful position her boss had put him in and the difficult choice he'd had to make. "Jake shouldn't be allowed to manipulate us this way."

"In his mind, he's saving you from the same man who stole his sister away and let her die."

"Hailey's death was an accident. You couldn't prevent what happened."

"Not the accident itself. But I'm the one who wanted to compete in the team penning event that day. Hailey was pregnant and had no business being on a horse."

"Did you ask her to compete with you?"

"Of course not. She went behind my back and signed up with some friends of ours."

"Hailey was always very determined. Nobody influenced her decisions. Not even Jake." Natalie wanted to say she was like Hailey in that respect but refrained. There had been too many comparisons recently between the two of them.

"I should have stayed home. She wouldn't have gone if not for me."

At the rough catch in Aaron's voice, she turned and looked at him for the first time since they'd sat down on the steps. His red-rimmed eyes and closed features spoke volumes.

Guilt—over his wife's death more than Jake's bullying—was the reason Aaron planned on leaving in the morning. He was afraid of endangering her and Shiloh. And Jake, whether intentionally or not, constantly reminded Aaron of his failure to take proper care of his wife and unborn child.

"What if we lie low for a month or two? Then you can come back." Now that she understood Aaron, and what she was fighting, she could find a solution.

"It's not that simple." He rubbed her arm, much the way a parent might comfort a child who was too young to grasp what was happening.

"I don't want to lose you."

"You have no idea how much it means to me to hear you say that." He closed his eyes momentarily and drew a breath. "But your home is here. You said so yourself, if you ever got to travel, you'd always return to Bear Creek Ranch."

"Ending things between us isn't the answer either." She felt as if a terrible weight was pressing down on her, robbing her lungs of their ability to function.

"A lot can happen in a year."

Platitudes. She hated them. "You're afraid of commitment. Admit it."

"You may be right." He rested his elbows on his knees. "I can't risk hurting you like I did Hailey."

"That's a cop-out, Aaron."

He didn't contradict her.

She was suddenly furious. Guilt over Hailey's death, okay. She could buy that. A feeling of responsibility toward her, also okay. Aaron wouldn't intentionally hurt others. But this fear that history would repeat itself was absurd.

"What's with you and Jake?" She pulled away from him and

pushed to her feet. "I'm not Hailey. Don't treat me like her. Don't confuse me with her."

"It's hard not to sometimes."

Of everything he'd said in the last hour, that cut the deepest. She'd been fooling herself all along, thinking what she and Aaron had was special and unique and worth fighting for.

"Leave."

"Natalie."

She pointed at his truck. "Now."

He stood. "What do you want from me?"

"If you don't know, then I guess you've got till next February to figure it out."

She was on the verge of tears. Worse, her mother had come out from her cabin next door and was staring at them. She probably wondered why Natalie hadn't come over to fetch Shiloh.

Aaron noticed Natalie's mother, too. "I'll call you later tonight," he said and reached for her.

"Don't." She stepped back and glared at him. "Don't call, don't come over. Just go." Her dictate sounded vaguely familiar. Then she remembered. She'd told Drew almost the same thing.

And like Drew, Aaron complied.

Hugging herself, Natalie watched him get into his truck and drive away. Her throat burned, and her eyes swam. She needed a few minutes alone before going to her mother's. Stumbling up the steps, she pushed open the door.

Not again.

Once inside the house, her tears fell in earnest. Aaron's fear that history would repeat itself wasn't absurd at all. Hadn't she just proved it?

TAN WORK SLACKS and a pair of dusty, worn work boots entered Aaron's line of vision, disrupting his packing. He looked up to find Skunk standing over him.

His bunkmate and friend tugged out his iPod earplugs and heaved a sad sigh.

In eight weeks, Aaron had become adept at reading Skunk's body language. "I can't stay. But I'll be back."

Skunk tilted his head to one side.

"Next year."

He frowned.

"We went through this already." Aaron had waited until that morning to tell Skunk, Rick and Teresa he was leaving. He gave the job with Air Waves Communications as his excuse, omitting the part about Natalie and their breakup.

His bunkmates were surely smart enough to figure out more was going on than what they were being told, but didn't ask.

Skunk tapped a booted foot and glowered at Aaron.

"Forget it, baby." Teresa came up behind Skunk. "No use talking to him. He's done got the itch to go and ain't nothing you say is gonna stop him."

He hung his head.

Teresa patted him sympathetically on the back. "Yeah, well, he's gonna miss us, too."

Aaron felt like a heel.

Rick came out of the shower a minute later, hair wet, shirt untucked and a clean pair of socks in his hand. "You're blowing it big-time, pal. Natalie's a hell of a girl."

Rather than eat breakfast in the dining hall, Aaron's bunkmates decided to stick around to try to talk some sense into him. Though no one said they were hungry, Skunk and Teresa toasted bread and poured glasses of juice.

Aaron would, he decided, have one last meal with his friends. He'd miss them. He'd miss Natalie a whole lot more.

When his bunkmates could no longer postpone heading to work, Aaron carried his duffel bag to his truck. Teresa would ride with him down to the stables.

"Goodbye." Skunk gave Aaron a hug. For a man of few words, he managed to say an awful lot.

Rick hugged Aaron next while Teresa sniffed and rubbed her nose with the back of her hand. He'd said farewell to a lot of close friends during the years he rodeoed. It wasn't something he'd ever grow used to.

Natalie must have told her parents something of what went on yesterday. When Aaron arrived at the stables, Gary kept his distance, busying himself with one chore after another. Only when Aaron was ready to load Dollar did Gary say anything.

"I'd've quit the ranch."

"Now you don't have to." Aaron had backed his truck up to his horse trailer and was securing the hitch.

Gary stood beside him, watching. "Natalie's having a tough go of it now, but eventually she'll see that everything worked out for the best."

If everything worked out for the best, why did it seem to Aaron that he was making the biggest mistake of his life?

"Don't worry, son," Gary said. "Natalie's mother and I will help her get through this."

Like they had the last time? Aaron wished Gary would be less agreeable and maybe punch his lights out instead. He deserved it for becoming just what Natalie had before and didn't need again: a good-for-nothing cowboy afraid of commitment.

Grabbing a halter, Aaron lead Dollar from his stall to the trailer. Apparently, the horse didn't want to leave either, because he refused the first few times Aaron tried to load him.

Gary shook Aaron's hand when he'd finished latching the trailer door behind Dollar. "See you next year."

Everyone kept saying the same thing. *See you next year.* Aaron wasn't so sure he wanted to return. Not if he couldn't be with Natalie. The long separation might mellow Jake, though Aaron doubted it. His ex-brother-in-law had a memory like a steel trap.

If it weren't for the foundation and the money from the trust… Wait. Now that he thought about it, he didn't need the trust to fund the foundation. Air Waves Communications had promised a sizable annual donation as part of their job offer, and with his connections, he could easily solicit more.

It occurred to him as he passed Natalie's cabin that there might be something else he could do with his share of the trust. Something that would atone for the hurt he'd caused her.

Stopping in the parking lot where the signal was better, he took out his cell phone and called Howard, the family trust attorney. He wasn't in his office yet so Aaron left a lengthy voice-mail message, outlining his instructions in detail.

He placed a second call to Trinkets and Treasures. Millie had been his one friend among the Tuckers, and he hated to leave without saying goodbye to her. The store didn't open for two more hours, so he left word saying he'd stop by then.

Putting the truck in gear, he rolled through the main gate and left Bear Creek Ranch, for what would be the last time if all went as planned. His one consolation was the knowledge he'd done the right thing.

"NATALIE, GET IN HERE," Jake called from his office.

"Coming." She dabbed at the corners of her eyes with a tissue.

Why she bothered she didn't know. Jake would take one look at her and know she'd spent the night crying. She'd contemplated calling in sick this morning, but the prospect of being alone and miserable appealed to her less than being at work. Here, at least, she'd be occupied and only think of Aaron every other second instead of continuously.

She'd hoped Jake wouldn't be in the office today, preferring not to see him until after she'd reconciled her feelings. He might have meant well by what he did yesterday, but that didn't excuse his actions. Later, when she was up to it emotionally, they'd have to talk.

"Howard's on the speakerphone," Jake said the instant she entered his office and indicated for her to take a seat. "He says he has a matter to discuss with us."

"*Both* of us?" That made no sense. What could the family trust attorney want with her? With her *and Jake?*

"Hello, Natalie," Howard said from the speakerphone.

"Good morning." She looked questioningly from Jake to the phone.

"What's going on, Howard?" Jake stood behind his desk, occasionally pacing back and forth. The lines of fatigue on his face evidenced he, too, had slept poorly the previous night.

"Aaron left a message on my phone this morning regarding his shares in the trust. Do either of you know anything about this or where he is? I've tried calling his cell, and he's not answering."

"No," Jake answered and resumed pacing.

"Me neither," Natalie said, more confused than ever. "Other than he's going back to Phoenix."

"What's this all about?" Jake paused long enough to take a sip of coffee from the mug on his desk.

"Aaron left instructions for me to draw up the paperwork necessary for him to transfer his share of the family trust to another individual. Which is why I asked to speak with you, Natalie."

"He's assigning his shares to me?"

"No, your daughter, Shiloh."

"You're not serious!" Her total and complete shock was mirrored on Jake's face.

"Can he do that?" Jake yanked his chair out and sat down.

"Shares in the trust can only be transferred to a parent, sibling, spouse or child. Legal child. Aaron would have to adopt Shiloh."

"Has he ever discussed adoption with you?" Jake asked Natalie.

"Absolutely not!" They'd never even discussed marriage.

"Well, it's a grand gesture for sure," Howard said. "But not possible."

Natalie was too wrapped up in her own thoughts to hear the rest of Jake's conversation with Howard. She still couldn't believe it. Aaron wanted to give Shiloh his share of the Tucker Family Trust. Nobody gave away something worth…oh my God…hundreds of thousands of dollars.

"He must really care about Shiloh." Jake had hung up with Howard and was studying Natalie intently. "And you."

"He must."

Maybe he even loved her. It would explain why he'd left and why he'd tried to make amends. And why, if she was the least bit smart, she wouldn't let him get away.

She sprang from the chair, her heart hammering. "I have to go."

"Where?" Jake asked.

Her decision was instantaneous. "Laveen." If Aaron wasn't at his mother's home, she might know where Natalie could find him.

"I'll have Alice pull his address for you. How much time do you need off?"

She stood, her hand on the back of the chair. "You're not mad?"

He exhaled a long breath. "Before Howard phoned, I'd intended to apologize to you. I was wrong to come between you and Aaron and wrong to threaten you with your job."

"You *were* wrong."

"It wasn't a conclusion I came to until about three this morning after a great deal of soul-searching."

"I had one of those nights myself." Natalie appreciated Jake's confession. He didn't often admit he was wrong.

"I've been blaming Aaron for my own mistakes, my own shortcomings. Where Hailey was concerned and this ranch. In the last three weeks, he's affected a change that I haven't been able to accomplish in the last three years. That's a hard pill for me to swallow."

"You two would make far better partners than adversaries."

"I'm not quite ready for that," Jake said on a derisive chuckle, then continued more thoughtfully. "What he did this morning for Shiloh, or tried to do, that was nice. Not what I expected of him."

"Me neither."

"It has me doubting my convictions. If I was wrong about

blaming him for my mistakes, I might have been wrong about one or two other things where he's concerned."

"Like?" Natalie could see the changes in Jake, a softening in his demeanor. He looked more like the old Jake, the one she enjoyed working for and had been friends with her whole life.

"Like his feelings for you. Nobody gives away something as valuable as part ownership in this ranch to someone they don't love."

Natalie smiled, her spirits suddenly soaring. "I was just thinking the same thing myself."

Alice burst into the office. "Millie's on the line. She said Aaron's at the store and that he doesn't know she called us."

"Tell her to do whatever it takes to keep him there for the next thirty minutes." Jake returned Natalie's smile. "Well, what are you waiting for? Get going."

She didn't need to be told twice. Five minutes later, she was in her car and speeding to Payson.

NATALIE PULLED into an empty parking space in front of Trinkets and Treasures. She caught a glimpse of Aaron's truck and trailer parked in the back of the store. Jumping from her car, she tore through the front entrance.

"Aaron," she called. "Where are you?" Walking on tiptoe, she peered over the tops of tall bookcases and shelving units. "Aaron. Millie. Anybody home?"

"Here."

Natalie followed the sound of Millie's voice.

She met up with Natalie at the rear door to the store. "I have him moving some furniture in and out of the storage room. I didn't want him to see you until you arrived."

"Thanks." She gave Millie a quick hug and dashed outside.

The storage room was actually a portable aluminum shed sitting against the rear wall of the building. Several pieces of small furniture sat on the ground outside the open door. Aaron must be inside.

Every nerve in Natalie's body vibrated with anticipation, yet she slowed her steps. What would he say when he saw her? What would he do?

Seconds later he emerged from the shed, and she had her answers.

"Natalie!" He came to an abrupt standstill. First shock and then relief registered on his face. No, joy.

She needed no other incentive.

"What in the world were you thinking, transferring your share of the trust to Shiloh?" She tried her best to sound mad. Grinning from ear to ear probably minimized the effect. "Are you insane? That's worth a ton of money."

"It seemed like the right thing to do." He inched toward her.

She did the same. "You can't, you know. Not that I would have let you. Howard called. He said shares can only be transferred to parents, siblings, spouses or legal children."

"Guess I should have read the fine print first. Or…"

"Or what?" They were only a few feet apart.

He removed his cowboy hat and tossed it onto a nearby antique step stool. "Proposed."

"Really?" The next thing she knew, she was in his arms, and he was hugging her as if he couldn't bear to let her go.

"I've been here for over an hour. Not because Millie needs help but because I can't make myself leave without you."

"All you had to do was ask."

"I wanted to. Thought a lot about it. But then Jake threatened to fire you. Leaving your job is a choice. Losing it, something else altogether."

"Maybe it took almost losing my job for me to realize there was something else I wanted a whole lot more."

"So, is that a yes? Or should I get down on one knee?"

"I don't want you anywhere but right here." She pressed her cheek to his chest and listened to his heart. Its accelerated rhythm matched her own. "Don't leave. Stay at Bear Creek Ranch and marry me."

He groaned in frustration. "The foundation board meeting is next week. I can't postpone it again."

"I'll come with you. As long as I get to meet your family."

"My mother would disown me if I didn't bring you by for a long visit." He drew back to look at her. "What about Jake? If he tries to—"

"He won't do anything. Believe me. He's had a change of heart. In fact, I wouldn't be surprised if he talked with you about another event like the breakfast ride."

Aaron laughed. "This I have to see." He tucked a finger under her chin and lifted her gaze to his. "There's still the matter of the trust to settle."

"How so?"

"I want to adopt Shiloh so that I can legally transfer my share when the time is right."

"Oh, Aaron." He really did always know the right thing to say. "I don't care about the trust or your money."

"I know that, *querida*. If you did care, I wouldn't love you so much."

"I love you, too." She angled her head and brought her mouth to his.

He pulled back just out of reach. "There's one more thing."

"What?" She sifted her fingers through the hair at his temple.

"Two tickets for a cruise to Hawaii. Think your boss will give you the time off work?"

"A cruise?"

"A honeymoon. We can take Shiloh?"

"Do you mean it?"

"After the board meeting next week, I don't ever want to be apart from either of you again."

"Aaron." Enough waiting. She pressed her lips to his in a heated kiss. Only last night, her life had looked so bleak. Today, everything she'd ever wanted, ever dreamed of, was coming true. One impossibly grand, completely impossible, gesture had changed everything.

They might have continued kissing if not for Millie. Her loud throat clearing let them know they were no longer alone.

"Looks like I'm going to be pretty busy the next few months." She stood by the back door, a huge sunny smile on her face.

"Doing what?" Natalie asked, unable to contain the laughter bubbling up inside her.

Millie came toward them, her arms outstretched and ready to embrace the both of them. "Planning the biggest wedding Bear Creek Ranch has ever seen."

* * * * *

For the next book in our
THE STATE OF PARENTHOOD *miniseries,*
we're heading east to Georgia in Tanya Michaels's
A DAD FOR HER TWINS.
Turn the page for a sneak peek,
and watch as single mom Kenzie Green moves
into a new neighborhood...and meets
the mysterious J.T. for the first time.

"Need help?" The man addressing Kenzie had an intriguing voice—sort of low and growly, yet not unpleasant.

His tone, though, was laced with so much skepticism, as if she was *clearly* beyond help, that Kenzie wondered why he'd offered. Maybe it just seemed like the thing to do since she, a torn cardboard box and all of the box's former contents blocked his path. Her groan stemmed from equal parts embarrassment and sore muscles.

Glancing up from her sprawled position in the stairwell, she got her first good look at the potential knight in paint-stained armor. Paint-stained denim and cotton, if you wanted to be literal. Which she did. The new-and-improved practical Kenzie couldn't afford flights of fancy.

Then stop staring at this guy as if he's the physical embodiment of your fantasies.

Frankly, it had been too long since she'd had a decent fantasy, but if she had, it would look like him. Thick dark hair, silver-gray eyes, strong jaw and broad, inviting shoulders. None of which were as relevant as the fact that she was still on her butt. She got to her feet…more or less.

As if she were having an out-of-body experience, she watched her wet sneaker slide across a piece of debris as she fell backward. The handsome stranger grabbed her elbow. Large hands, roughened skin. Since he was theoretically saving her from an ignominious death in a dingy stairwell, she could forgive the lack of delicate touch. The way her luck was running this morning, she would have broken her neck if he hadn't come along.

The man shook his head. "Lady." Was the undertone exasperation or amusement? Hard to tell from the single word.

"It's Kenzie," she said, grabbing the stair rail with both hands. "Kenzie Green. And thank you."

"No problem." He'd stepped back, either to keep from crushing her belongings under his work boots or simply to avoid her rain-soaked aura of doom.

She grimaced at the mess that covered half a dozen stairs. The coasters she was always admonishing the kids to use. Assorted books, her texts from some correspondence courses alongside Leslie's Mary Pope Osborne stories. Two mauve lamp shades. A statuette of a now-headless panda Kenzie had once received for donating to a wildlife fund and various other small belongings that had been packed, taped up and neatly labeled LIVING ROOM in black marker.

"Guess they don't make cardboard boxes like they used to," she grumbled. What was wrong with the stupid box that it couldn't withstand being weakened with water and dropped down a few lousy steps?

Thank goodness Kenzie was such a levelheaded pragmatist. If she were given to the slightest bit of paranoia or superstition, she might see it as a bad sign that her first summer day in the sunny South was under deluge from a monsoon. She might be rethinking that rent check she'd written to a place where the elevator doors wouldn't even open.

"Are you the handyman?" she asked suddenly, taking in the man's clothing and an almost chemical smell she hadn't initially noticed. A cleaner of some kind, or paint? Maybe the elevator would be fixed before Ann arrived with the kids. Not that Drew couldn't take three flights of stairs in a single breath, but he hardly needed new reasons to complain.

"The handyman?" Tall, Dark and Timely let out a bark of

laughter that was gone as soon as it came. In fact, all traces of amusement disappeared from his expression so quickly she wondered if she'd imagined them.

"I'll take that as a no," she said. "It was an educated guess— Mr. Carlyle assured me that a handyman would be taking care of the elevators today. Which would make moving in a lot easier."

"Mr. C. *is* the handyman, in addition to being the property manager and the one who knocks on the doors whenever you're late with rent."

She stiffened. "I'm never late with rent."

He raised an eyebrow at her hostile tone. "I meant in general."

"Sorry. I take money seriously."

"You and everyone else." He grimaced absently, as if he was scowling at an unseen person. Did he owe someone money?

Oh, don't let him be one of those charming but perpetually broke deadbeats. There were too many of those in the world already. Then again, this guy wasn't technically all that charming. Hot, definitely, but not so much with the personality.

Imagining how Leslie would react to her mother calling a man hot, Kenzie grinned. "Well, thanks again. It was nice to almost meet you."

The corner of his lips quirked. "I'm J.T. Good luck with the rest of your move." He started to pass, but stopped, watching as she wrestled with the lamp shades and books. With the box no longer intact, carting her belongings was problematic.

"I hate to impose," she began, "but were you in a hurry? It's going to take me a couple of trips to haul everything to the third floor, and if you wouldn't mind sticking around in the meantime to make sure no one…" What, stole her stuff? Who would want the book of *101 Jokes for Number Crunchers* Drew got her last Christmas? "To make sure no one trips. I'd hate to be sued my first day in the city."

"I have a better idea." He was already sweeping up an armful of debris. After years of not having a guy in the household, it seemed bizarrely intimate to see this big man handle her possessions.

Books, Kenzie, not lingerie. Besides, people with better budgets than hers hired strangers to move their stuff all the time.

J.T. gestured toward the decapitated panda. "You keeping this poor fellow?"

"Sure. That's what they make glue for, right?" A couple of drops of that super all-stick compound and, as long as she managed not to chemically bond her fingers together, the panda should be as good as new.

Using the soggy cardboard in a way that reminded her of the baby sling she'd bought Ann, J.T. cradled the awkward bulk against his body. Between the two of them, they got it all up to her floor.

There were four units, two on each side of the hallway. Hers was the last on the left. As she unlocked her door, she heard J.T.'s slight intake of breath, as if he was about to say something, but nothing followed. So she set down her load, turned to relieve him of his and thanked him one last time.

"I've got it from here," she said, hoping she sounded like a confident, self-sufficient woman.

"You sure?"

She thought about everything ahead, the new job, this temporary moving before the *real* move, trying to keep the kids from expiring boredom until school started and trying to keep them in their teachers' good graces once it did.

"Absolutely," she lied through her teeth. Next time she lectured the twins never to fib, she'd have to add the mental exception *unless it's the only thing between you and a nervous breakdown.*

* * * * *

The Colton family is back!
Enjoy a sneak preview of
COLTON'S SECRET SERVICE
by Marie Ferrarella,
part of
THE COLTONS: FAMILY FIRST *miniseries.*

Available from Silhouette Romantic Suspense
in September 2008.

He cautioned himself to be leery. He was human and he'd been conned before. But never by anyone nearly so attractive. Never by anyone he'd felt so attracted to.

In her defense, Nick supposed that Georgie could actually be telling him the truth. That she was a victim in all this. He had his people back in California checking her out, to make sure she was who she said she was and had, as she claimed, not even been near a computer but on the road these last few months that the threats had been made.

In the meantime, he was doing his own checking out. Up close and exceedingly personal. So personal he could feel his blood stirring.

It had been a long time since he'd thought of himself as anything other than a law enforcement agent of one type or other. But Georgeann Grady made him remember that beneath the oaths he had taken and his devotion to duty, there beat the heart of a man.

A man who'd been far too long without the touch of a woman.

He watched as the light from the fireplace caressed the outline of Georgie's small, trim, jean-clad body as she moved about the rustic living room that could have easily come off the set of a Hollywood Western. Except that it was genuine.

As genuine as she claimed to be?

Something inside of him hoped so.

He wasn't supposed to be taking sides. His only interest in being here was to guarantee Senator Joe Colton's safety as the latter continued to make his bid for the presidency. Everything else was supposed to be secondary, but, Nick had to silently admit, that was just a wee bit hard to remember right now.

Earlier, before she'd put her precocious handful of a daughter to bed, Georgie had fed his appetite by whipping up some kind of a delicious concoction out of the vegetables she'd pulled from her garden. Vegetables that, by all rights, should have been withered and dried. She'd mentioned that a friend came by on occasion to weed and tend it. Still, it surprised him that somehow she'd managed to make something mouthwatering out of it.

Almost as mouthwatering as she looked to him right at this moment.

Again, he was reminded of the appetite that hadn't been fed, hadn't been satisfied.

And wasn't going to be, Nick sternly told himself. At least not now. Maybe later, when things took on a more definite shape and all the questions in his head were answered to his satisfaction, there would be time to explore this feeling. This woman. But not now.

Damn it.

"Sorry about the lack of light," Georgie said, breaking into his train of thought as she turned around to face him. If she noticed the way he was looking at her, she gave no indication. "But I don't see a point in paying for electricity if I'm not going to be here. Besides, Emmie really enjoys camping out. She likes roughing it."

"And you?" Nick asked, moving closer to her, so close that a whisper would have trouble fitting in. "What do you like?"

The very breath stopped in Georgie's throat as she looked up at him.

"I think you've got a fair shot of guessing that one," she told him softly.

* * * * *

Be sure to look for
COLTON'S SECRET SERVICE
and the other following titles from
THE COLTONS: FAMILY FIRST *miniseries:*

RANCHER'S REDEMPTION
by Beth Cornelison
THE SHERIFF'S AMNESIAC BRIDE
by Linda Conrad
SOLDIER'S SECRET CHILD
by Caridad Piñeiro
BABY'S WATCH
by Justine Davis
A HERO OF HER OWN
by Carla Cassidy

Silhouette®

Romantic
SUSPENSE

Sparked by Danger, Fueled by Passion.

The Coltons Are Back!

Marie Ferrarella
Colton's Secret Service

The Coltons: Family First

On a mission to protect a senator, Secret Service agent
Nick Sheffield tracks down a threatening message only
to discover Georgie Gradie Colton, a rodeo-riding single
mom, who insists on her innocence. Nick is instantly
taken with the feisty redhead, but vows not to let his
feelings interfere with his mission. Now he must figure
out if this woman is conning him or if he can trust her
and the passion they share....

Available September wherever books are sold.

**Look for upcoming Colton titles
from Silhouette Romantic Suspense:**

RANCHER'S REDEMPTION by Beth Cornelison, Available October
THE SHERIFF'S AMNESIAC BRIDE by Linda Conrad, Available November
SOLDIER'S SECRET CHILD by Caridad Piñeiro, Available December
BABY'S WATCH by Justine Davis, Available January 2009
A HERO OF HER OWN by Carla Cassidy, Available February 2009

Visit Silhouette Books at www.eHarlequin.com   SRS27598

NEW YORK TIMES BESTSELLING AUTHOR

SUSAN WIGGS

With her marriage in the rearview mirror, Sarah flees to her hometown, a place she couldn't wait to leave. Now she finds herself revisiting the past—a distant father and the unanswered questions left by her mother's death. As she comes to terms with her lost marriage, Sarah encounters a man she never expected to meet again: Will Bonner, her high-school heartthrob. Now a local firefighter, he's been through some changes himself. But just as her heart opens, Sarah discovers she is pregnant—with her ex's twins.

It's hardly the most traditional of new beginnings, but who says life or love are predictable...or perfect?

Just Breathe

"Susan Wiggs paints the details of human relationships with the finesse of a master."
—*New York Times* bestselling author Jodi Picoult

Available the first week of September 2008 wherever hardcovers are sold!

MIRA®

REQUEST YOUR FREE BOOKS!

2 FREE NOVELS PLUS 2
FREE GIFTS!

Heart, Home & Happiness!

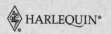

Inside ROMANCE

Stay up-to-date on all your romance reading news!

The Inside Romance newsletter is a FREE quarterly newsletter highlighting our upcoming series releases and promotions!

Click on the <u>Inside Romance</u> link on the front page of **www.eHarlequin.com** or e-mail us at insideromance@harlequin.ca to sign up to receive your FREE newsletter today!

You can also subscribe by writing us at: HARLEQUIN BOOKS Attention: Customer Service Department P.O. Box 9057, Buffalo, NY 14269-9057

Please allow 4-6 weeks for delivery of the first issue by mail.

IRNBPA208

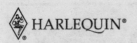

HARLEQUIN®

American ★ Romance®

COMING NEXT MONTH

#1225 A DAD FOR HER TWINS by Tanya Michaels
The State of Parenthood
Kenzie Green is starting over—new job, new city, new house—to provide a better life for her nine-year-old twins. Unfortunately, the house isn't finished yet, so the three of them temporarily move into an apartment across the hall from the mysterious and gorgeous Jonathan Trelauney. Watching her kids open up to JT is enthralling...thinking of him as a father to her twins is irresistible!

#1226 TEXAS HEIR by Linda Warren
Cari Michaels has been in love with the newly engaged Reed Preston, CEO and heir to a family-owned Texas chain of department stores, for a long time. When their plane crashes in desolate west Texas—and help doesn't arrive—they start the long trek to civilization. Once they're rescued, will Reed follow through with his engagement...or marry the woman who has captured his heart?

#1227 SMOKY MOUNTAIN HOME by Lynnette Kent
Ruth Ann Blakely has worked in the stables at The Hawksridge School for most of her life. Her attachment to the students she teaches, to her horses and to the stables themselves is unshakeable. So when architect Jonah Granger is hired to build new a stable for the school—and tear the old one down—he's in for a fight. But Jonah isn't a man who's easy to say no to....

#1228 A FIREFIGHTER IN THE FAMILY by Trish Milburn
When Miranda "Randi" Cooke is assigned to investigate a fire in her hometown, she not only has to face her estranged family but also her ex-boyfriend Zac Parker. As the case heats up, Randi finds she needs Zac's help. While they're working closely together, her feelings for Zac are rekindled—but can the tough arson investigator forgive old hurts and learn to trust again?

www.eHarlequin.com

HARCNM0808